KILLER STORM

Sue & Steve —

   Thanks so much for being an ally. I know you know how much it means.

Jenn Wright
6/07

KILLER STORM

A Jo Spence Mystery

Jen Wright

CLOVER VALLEY PRESS, LLC
DULUTH, MINNESOTA

Clover Valley Press, LLC
6286 Homestead Rd.
Duluth, MN 55804-9621
USA

This is a work of fiction. Any resemblance between characters in this book and actual persons, living or dead, is coincidental.

Cover design by Sally Rauschenfels

Printed in the United States of America on acid-free paper

Library of Congress Control Number: 2007926425

ISBN-13: 978-0-9794883-0-6
ISBN-10: 0-9794883-0-3

Acknowledgments

I WOULD LIKE to thank the following people for their invaluable contributions to this book:

Charlene Brown, I can't list here how much you gave to me in this process. Your mentorship as a writer and editor is a precious gift. Without your encouragement and guidance, I would never have had the courage to complete this book. You improved the quality tenfold with writing tips and editing. Thank you so much.

To my life partner, Kari Gastler: Remember when you read the entire book to me out loud, and we figured out where the writing could flow better? Thank you for all of the ways that you supported me through this process. You are the best!

Thank you, Officer Scott Jenkins from the Duluth Police Department, for your gang and Drug Task Force knowledge; Ericka Eberhart, Ph.D., for your dream analysis contribution; Char Applewick, probation officer, for your careful reading, editing, and input regarding probation matters; Holly Johnson for your editing and encouragement; Becky Pogatchnik, probation officer, for your careful reading and editing; Maggie Jezierski for content editing; Karen Olson for catching repeated words; Helen Mongan-Rallis, Ph.D., University of Minnesota Duluth, for input regarding university realism; and Joan M. Drury for title and opening scene suggestions.

To Ruby Horn (Grandma Horn)
for loving me unconditionally
when I needed it most

Chapter 1

I PADDLED OUR CANOE through glasslike water. The sun, high in a cloudless sky, felt warm on my face. My best friend, Kathy, had taken her shirt off and was resting her back on her Duluth pack in the bow of the boat, with a huge smile on her face. I let the boat drift toward our remote campsite in the BWCA.

"Hey duffer, slacking off already?" I couldn't resist teasing her.

"I'm working on my technique here, and I think it is nearly as good as yours."

Just as I eased into shore, a discordant sound rang through the air. I jerked awake, my heart pounding in my chest.

"Jo Spence." I said into my cell phone, realizing as I said it that it was how I answered the phone at work, where I am Duluth's Juvenile Probation Supervisor. My eyes were barely focusing, but I could see that it was 2:49 A.M.

"Jo, it's Nate. We have a problem involving Lou and your agency."

"I'm all ears." I tried to sound calm.

"No, I can't go into it on the phone. I mean, aah ... can you come in?"

"Of course, where are you?"

"Let's meet at your office. Can you be there in twenty minutes?"

"Twenty-five. But Nate, give me something here. It's the middle of the night. It's bad, right?"

"I can't say more right now, Jo. This is not a secure line. I'm really sorry."

I changed, kenneled the dogs, took one longing look at my coffeepot, and sped to work. En route, I wondered if this was the situation I had always dreaded. Something really bad had happened to one of my staff.

OK, I thought. Possible scenarios were (1) Lou was injured or killed, (2) another probation officer had done something stupid, and Lou had intervened, or (3) shit, I don't know what else.

Dealing with the struggles of our troubled youth was stressful enough, but worrying about the safety of my staff sometimes put me right over the edge. I had never quite adjusted to the helpless feeling of overseeing rather than doing.

The drive in seemed endless. Up until that moment, I had not considered my home in the Valley to be anything but an asset. Living just outside the city limits of Duluth fit well with my love of the outdoors and recreational activities. Plus, I had always found the thirty-minute commute to be a nice, relaxing buffer between my distinctly different home and work lives. On this drive, however, it was anything but an asset. When I'm stressed, I need to move. I ski, walk, shovel, build something, or clean like a madwoman. Anything but sit.

I reached into my pocket and retrieved a small, smooth stone that I had picked up on one of my outdoor adventures. I often carry just such a rock and rub it in stressful situations. I touched my rock and felt a little more grounded. I believe I was close to sane when I finally pulled up to our meeting spot.

Nate, a.k.a. Sergeant Jerome Nathan, was waiting in a squad car in the back parking lot behind my building. I quickly got out of my vehicle and approached.

"What, Nate? This is killing me."

"OK. Here in the squad, then." He motioned for me to join him inside. Pausing, he tried to formulate words. "The Toivunen family has been murdered. All four of them are dead—mom, dad, and the two kids. They were shot execution style in their living room." He looked at me to see if what he was saying had fully registered.

"Jesus, Nate. How did you hear about it at this time of night? The shots?"

"No, they used silencers. We got an anonymous tip. I should say, you got an anonymous tip. They called your guy Lou at midnight. We went in together. It was pretty gruesome."

"Where is Lou now?"

"At the scene. Let's go."

As we pulled up in front of the Toivunen household, Lou was visible from a distance. I felt a rush of relief from the worry I had experienced on my drive in. I thought about my most senior—and if I had to be honest—my favorite probation officer, Lou Ornado. Looking at him is like being swept away by a piece of art that is so moving you can't speak. His part-Hispanic, part-Native mix is beautiful and perfect. He stands at a graceful six-foot, four inches tall, with dark wavy hair, deep brown eyes, long eyelashes, and a very fit body.

I took a minute to gather myself. I knew this would be an emotionally charged scene for Lou, and I really wanted to be there for him.

The Toivunen house was in the Central Hillside neighborhood of Duluth, a cluster of houses built into the hill just north of the downtown area. Recent census data had placed it among the top five most impoverished areas per capita in the country. The neighborhood includes mostly low-rent apartments with a few houses trying to maintain some dignity. The Toivunens lived in one of those houses. It was a narrow, three-story affair that was probably built at the turn of the century. Many of the well-cared-for homes had been handed down from the first immigrant generation, with homeowners trying to hang on, hoping that the Hillside would become gentrified. City planners had not addressed problems in the area even, with the recent declaration of poverty.

The first snow of the season had begun to fall. The house looked surreal. Oscillating red lights from the squads struggled to penetrate through the snow. Lou was standing out front smoking. He had quit the year before. I found myself craving my own favorite addiction, coffee. His face was stonelike and unreadable. To my knowledge, Lou had never been first on the scene of a murder.

"Lou. How are you?"

He nodded and looked at the house. "Hell of a thing that was." He took a drag, and the end of his cigarette turned red, then white, from his effort.

"If this is Nichols, he is one sick bastard. What does he think, this is going to get him a ticket out of detention? A fucking free pass?" He took another drag, dropped the butt, and stepped on it, grinding it hard into the sidewalk. "Maybe he plans to go out with a bang. We've got to get him moved to the jail. The thought of him in the same building with fourteen-year-old kids in there for a school fight disturbs the hell out of me. This guy needs to be in isolation. Now!"

"Wait a minute—Nichols?" I put my hand up to stop him. "Slow down here. You mean the kid up in detention for John Toivunen's murder?"

He gave me a look that I could only interpret to mean Duh. "This was his house," I said softly. He nodded slowly.

I raised my hand and nodded. "I'm on it."

I used my cell to wake up Superintendent Lynn Carter of the Detention Center at home. She assured me that she would have Nichols put on administrative segregation with all meals served in his room and one hour per day of isolated recreation under guard supervision. She promised to arrange a hearing to have him transferred him to the jail at the earliest opportunity.

When I informed Lou, he said, "I can handle the hearing, Jo."

"First tell me why they called you. Why do you think you got the tip?"

"I have no idea! It was weird. The caller said, 'Go see what you caused.' Like this was somehow my fault."

"It's not your fault, Lou, and I have no doubt you can handle this, but we have to be careful here. We can't have the public defenders claiming you have some vendetta against this kid because he targeted you. I still need you on the streets in case this is a gang thing. Even if Nichols is pulling strings, we need to find out who the puppets are. Who is carrying this out? This was a horrific act. Whoever did this is responsible for four murders." I caught myself in the rant and gave Lou a closer look. He looked solemn and glossy eyed. "Lou, what do you need right now? Can you go home and get some sleep?"

"No. Can we go somewhere and just talk this thing through?"

"Joyce's is open all night. I'll drive you in your car."

"I can drive." He must have thought I was treating him with kid gloves.

"OK, OK, but I need a ride. My Rover is at the office. I need to wake up Probation Chief Long with this. He'll need to be briefed for the media statement."

"Don't invite him!" Lou was adamant.

"I know, all right. He does see the good you do, you know."

"That's not my worry."

4

Joyce's is a converted 7-11 with little or no charm, reliant upon the after-hours crowd for the majority of its business. The place was nearly empty, and the coffee was dark and old. I put a five on the table and asked the waitress for a fresh pot.

"Lou, I need you to fill me in on the Toivunen murder. What was behind that?"

"Well, I think it was over a girl. Toivunen was a decent kid, you know. Played football, B student, wasn't into drugs or drinking that I knew about. He worked at Lakes Ten Theatres. Seventeen, in the prime of his youth, and a nice guy, too. He was the kind of kid I would've liked my daughter to date." Lou stared at his hands.

"He was dating a girl by the name of Felicia Green who was enrolled at Central. She was biracial, smart, and a looker. She used to be Nichols's girl, but she wanted out. Nichols tried to buy her with expensive gifts, and he downplayed the gang stuff, but she was scared of him. When she tried to break it off, he got really controlling. He bought her a cell phone and called her at all hours in an attempt to track her every movement. I suspect he threatened to kill her, or got violent. I'm betting she went to Toivunen because he was different from Nichols, and probably because she thought he would protect her."

"Where is she now?"

"I don't know. As soon as she gave her statement to the police, she was gone. She and her parents disappeared. The police think they just moved away. There are enough corroborating witnesses to the relationship that they won't need her for trial."

"You don't think something happened to her whole family, do you?"

"No. I think I remember someone seeing a moving van. Let's hope not. Jesus. I can talk to Nate about that."

Lou leaned back in his chair and in a nearly flat monotone described John Toivunen's murder. "Here is how his murder went down. Nichols walked up to the house on a Sunday morning at 9 A.M. Mrs. Toivunen came to the door, and Nichols asked for John. When John came to the door, Nichols shot him in the chest and walked away. As Mrs. Toivunen was trying to rouse John, she looked up to see that Nichols had come back. He was just standing there with wild eyes. He looked straight at her, flashed his stupid little gang sign, and told her that if she talked to anyone he would kill her. Then he walked slowly to his car and drove away. She reported it to the police; he was picked up; end of story."

"Which gang is he with, Lou?"

"They call themselves the Gangster Mob. They're new, but vicious." He shrugged. "Can you believe that shit? The police didn't have the Toivunen house under surveillance tonight because Nichols was in lockup."

Lou's eyes glossed over for a couple of seconds, and I wondered if he was seeing that whole family again. He blinked, seemed to shake off the thought, and went on.

"I can remember when Duluth had only gang wanna-be's. That wasn't so long ago, remember Jo?" I nodded. "The first real gang moved in about five years ago. We had an increase in crime, and it took us a full six months to identify it as gang related. Then we got the gang strike force. Half the cops who are not strike force members still don't think the gangs are that bad. This will certainly change all that."

"Lou, I want you to make this your focus. Find out who killed that family. How would you feel about being pulled out of the intensive unit to work on this full time with the gang strike force?"

"I'm there."

I saw a spark in his eyes, and I felt a little fear about sending him smack dab into the middle of such a big case. I sensed he really needed it, though.

"I want to see a list of the known associates of Nichols. I'm guessing it's slim at this point. Get together with the strike force, and put out the word that you're looking. You are the best PO we've got when it comes to gangs, and they need you, but please be careful. I'll arrange it with the Police Department under two conditions: Keep me informed, and play by the rules. This case is too important to get thrown out. Don't be a cowboy. Don't risk your life." I caught myself, realized that my list of rules could go on and on, and just kept going. "Review the policy and procedures on assisting the police. Get a bulletproof vest, and wear it in the shower, to bed, whatever."

"You won't regret this, Jo."

I looked at my favorite PO and thought, _I certainly hope not._

* * * *

By the time we had finished, it was 6:30 A.M., and I was wide awake from the coffee.

I had Lou drop me at the office, and I called Chief Long at home, informing him of the murders. He had just heard it on the news and told me that it was being played up as gang violence. He predicted that this would put the whole city in fear. We discussed how to deal with the media. If we sent the news stations copies of the Gangster Mob symbols, we could more quickly identify suspects but would run the risk of inciting vigilante justice. We agreed that this decision really needed to come from the Police Department, and Long asked me to call Chief of Police Knight as soon as his office opened.

The press release was aired on all four of Duluth's local channels throughout the day. Knight respected my request to downplay Lou's involvement for his safety. The news described the horrific event and went on to say that the Probation Office and the Police Department were working around the clock to round up this gang. Knight was shown expressing his intent that the streets of Duluth would soon be safe. He came off as strong and confident, while sensitive to the extended Toivunen family.

The authorization for Lou to work with the police went smoothly. They were grateful for the help. On our end, though, I had to swear on my dogs' lives that Lou would not carry a gun, would only act as a consultant, and would play by the rules. I also had to transfer one of the standard desk PO's into the intensive unit, and that would go over like a ton of bricks. The staff would want time lines. Yeah, right.

I made some calls to the PO's at home and was pleasantly surprised when one of the older PO's from the felony unit volunteered. Warren Gott had become less involved with his fellow PO's in recent years, but he still must have felt some remnant of commitment to the agency.

Lou had to go through a critical incident debriefing, which would be conducted by an outside agency later that day. He was first on the scene of a grisly murder. As his immediate supervisor, I was required to attend with him. I was moved by how well he handled it. He talked freely about what it was like to walk up to that family.

"Their bodies were just shells," he said. "The people were gone." He admitted thinking about the fear they must have felt and how it must have been horrible to watch their loved ones killed one by one. Besides acknowledging that he was thinking about the murders from time to time, he also disclosed that he was worried about the safety of his family. I was impressed. I expected him to do some macho "I'm fine" thing. The therapist declared him fit for duty and gave him the name of a confidential counselor to call if he needed to talk more. We both left for home early in hopes of winding down enough to get some much needed sleep.

By then, my poor dogs had been out for twelve hours. I looked forward to the welcome home routine they go through every day when I arrive. They bound out of their matching overstuffed chairs, and then out of their heated shack. They run parallel to my truck along the six-foot-high fence until they come to the end just west of the garage. They wait sitting up and perfectly still to see if I am going to open the gate. At my first gesture toward the gate, they run, tails wagging, and jump up and down until they are free. The thought of that welcome always makes me smile.

My dogs were a little wound up when I got home, having missed their usual morning trail time, but I allowed myself a moment to let it all sink in before leading the way toward the trail behind my house.

It was a beautiful fall evening. My dogs were anxious to begin the walk. Cocoa howled a three-word dog sentence that I took to mean, "Thank you, thank you for this walk, and let's go right now." Java tried to look dignified, managed it for a full second, and then bounded after Cocoa.

I started to reflect on the day, caught myself, and focused instead on the smell of the trees, the damp cool earth, and the decay of the newly fallen leaves under a thin layer of snow. The few leaves that remained on the trees were bright orange and yellow. Those on the ground had begun to dry out, but the new snow made them cling to my hiking shoes as I walked along the trail. I contemplated which smell I loved more—the smell of the woods or of coffee. I cleared my mind again and enjoyed the walk.

Back in the house, I eased out of the same outfit that I wear to work virtually every day. Stain-resistant, permanent-press, khaki pants; a white long-sleeved T-shirt; and a sweater. In summer, I substitute a Pendlelton shirt in place of the sweater. The color and variety of sweaters change, but essentially that is my getup. I have twelve pairs of khakis, twelve sweaters, and twelve Pendletons. When they become worn, I rotate them into my leisure wear. My underwear of choice is a pair of black Jockey bikini briefs. I wear one pair of sensible, comfortable work shoes until they wear out. I have one pair of hiking boots and one pair of cross trainers. I don't own any makeup. I do indulge in liberal Aveda hair and aromatherapy products—my only wish is that they sold coffee-scented ones. I buy any earrings that I like and pay little or no attention to matching them with my clothing.

When I interviewed to promote from probation officer to Supervisor, I wore a very nice and very expensive suit. I half believe they gave me the job hoping to see a change in my wardrobe. Well, it didn't work. I think my staff finds comfort in my consistency. There is a slight chance I am projecting.

After turning on the gas fireplace in my bedroom, I slid into bed, had to nudge the dogs over to make enough space to get comfortable, and found myself drifting off to sleep.

Chapter 2

WHEN I OPENED MY eyes, the big green lights of my alarm clock read 5:58. Why did I always wake up just before my alarm? It was scheduled to go off at six o'clock. I lay there wondering why I couldn't go to bed without setting the damn thing. I knew I wouldn't oversleep, but something about my personality wouldn't let me trust my internal clock.

The green lights made me think of my ex, Dar. She bought that clock for me after many nights of watching me bolt straight up out of bed trying to put out the fire; the fire I saw starting in the corner of my room; the fire that was really just red lights. I wondered how long it took her to find this little green-lighted clock. Even though she was my ex by then, and the thought of her still pissed me off, I woke up liking her for this gift.

After six months of being single, I still woke up thinking about her. I wondered if I was abnormal somehow because I seemed to be stuck. Maybe I just needed to get another clock. I searched my mind for reasons why we had failed. Was it because she moved in with me after we'd been seeing each other for only a month? I thought about all of the arguments that we didn't have. Maybe we were just too different. She was laid back and never planned ahead. I pictured the pile of bills she paid only when the pile fell over. I pictured our home, cluttered with art projects, clothes, and empty cups. She cleaned when things got in the way and lived totally in the moment, a free spirit. By contrast, I knew my own tendency was to plan compulsively. I just couldn't function in any other way. I guess you could say that order has always been a comfort to me.

Neither one of us was good about "processing." I thought that was what being with a woman was supposed to be all about. Well, so far, in my twenty-plus years of exclusively seeing women, it had not proven true. I once read a self-help book on lesbian relationships that said we should avoid picking partners who we think are identical to or the opposite of ourselves. It seems I failed in this regard. I think I picked Dar to balance myself out and ended up resenting her for being herself. It ended badly.

On our last day together, we were supposed to go away for the weekend to share a cabin on the north shore of Lake Superior with our good friends Tina and Sally. I had my bag packed and loaded in the car before leaving for work. When it came time to go, Dar was on the phone organizing a hike with friends, having completely forgotten our plans. I spouted off about how unreliable she was and from there moved on to how our house wasn't a home; it was a dirty clothes pile. She just walked out, saying "Jo, I've had enough. I'll come back for my stuff while you're gone." I came home to an orderly and sparse house. I suspected that we would have dinner sometime, after a couple of messed up schedulings, and talk about the fact that we were just too different, or maybe about what an inflexible jerk I was.

The smell of coffee finally pulled me out of bed. I had programmed my pot to brew precisely two cups ready to drink by 5:55 A.M. I grabbed my mug, walked out to the deck, and began to sip. I wasn't too consumed with the thoughts in my head to hear the birds singing all around me. I tried to clear my mind, allowing nature to ground me before setting off on my ritual morning walk with my dogs. Before long, though, I found myself thinking about the Toivunen murders. I looked up midway on the trail and didn't know where I was. I half expected to be at the end by then. I gave up trying to clear my mind and hustled my dogs back to the house.

On the drive to Duluth, I glanced at my Palm Pilot, wondering how I could fit some time in my schedule to support Lou. I didn't even notice that the radio was off for the thirty-minute commute.

I rolled into a half-filled parking lot. It was the first week of deer hunting season, and most of the men in our office were sitting in tree stands. I entered my building, stomped off the leaves clinging to my shoes, and instinctively braced against the cold of the building where my office is located. Rumor has it that the city morgue used to be housed downstairs. If the rumor is true, the building had not lost the ambience. Originally built in the 1920s as a health clinic, it now housed a variety of businesses, including a Women's Health Center, psychologists' offices, and several nonprofit human service agencies. While the floors are a beautiful light marble and the ceilings twelve feet high, they don't compensate for the cold, clinical feel of the building. The plumbing and heating are original, and to make matters worse, building management turns the heat down at night and on weekends to save costs. In a cold snap, it takes a full two days before the temp. reaches 68 degrees. I pulled up my collar and hugged myself as a symbolic embrace against the cold. My soft shoes ticked off a staccato rhythm as I traversed the marble expanse to the stairwell leading to our third-floor offices.

The front office, originally designed as a waiting area, had had a fresh remodel, including a thermostatically controlled heating system all its own. Consequently, the clients waiting to see their probation officers experienced relative comfort compared to the rest of their visit.

Walking into the office, I noticed a fresh pile of baked goods on the front "treats table." Jeannie, our front desk supervisor, must have been busy baking the previous evening and didn't want to have the temptation at home. I quickly scanned the table for chocolate. Seeing nothing I couldn't live without, I gave a quick "good morning" to the front office staff, intending to catch up on their weekend activities later.

As I passed through the double security doors to my office, the disarray stunned me. I stared blankly. The room had been ransacked. A locked file cabinet containing all of the staff files was open. The drawer was bent outward as if someone had pried it from the outside. Paperwork was everywhere. My plants were turned over, and dirt was covering the paper, my desk, and the floor. All of the contents of my desk were on the floor. My burgundy leather chair was tipped over and leaning against the windowsill. I thought I could make out a light musky smell. My initial reaction of numbness and shock quickly turned to anger, and then to determination.

My prior training as Chief Security Officer at the juvenile detention facility kicked in. Secure the area, don't disturb anything, and memorize the scene. I moved to the neighboring office and called the front desk. I informed Jeannie that there had been a break-in and asked her not to allow anyone back and to please phone the police. I then moved to the security doors and diverted curious staff members until the police could arrive.

While I waited, I studied the doors. There was no sign of forced entry. The doors could be opened either with a magnetic security fob or by entering a numerical code into the keypad. The combinations on all of the door locks on the third floor are the same. It would be relatively easy for an offender to memorize the combination while his or her probation officer was opening the door from the waiting area. I was sure I had obliterated any fingerprints present on the keypad when I let myself in. I decided immediately that I would have to talk this over with the Chief of Probation and perhaps allow only fob operation in the presence of clients.

What the hell would someone want with my files? As head of Juvenile Probation, I hardly rank as a worthy target. Perhaps the intrusion was really about one of the probation officers. They do make recommendations to the court for sentencing on crimes involving drugs and even murder. What was this about? I couldn't help but tie it to the Toivunen murder somehow.

Damn, I had just done my annual weeding out of the piles of paperwork. Well, at least I had a better chance of knowing what was missing.

Jeannie escorted Nate down the hall. I felt myself smile in spite of the circumstances. Even with what happened the previous night, and what had just happened to my office, I thought about our first meeting fifteen years earlier. I had been working in the juvenile intensive unit, and he was a beat cop. I called for backup as I was trying to arrest one of the kids on my caseload for violating his probation by drinking. The kid was resisting, and his mother was in my face screaming at me. Nate rolled up in a squad and slowly walked up to us. We were in front of the house, and I'd been attempting to talk my client down so that I could place handcuffs on him. Nate walked up to the client, lumbered his six-foot, five-inch frame over him, and stuck out his hand as if to greet him. The kid didn't know what else to do, and shook his hand. Nate gave him a big smile and had him in cuffs within five seconds, all the while making small talk. The kid smiled and said, "Hey, smooth." Nate's head is small for his body, and his eyes are close together, but somehow the sight of him always makes me happy.

He approached me with his usual smile and handshake. "Jo."

"We meet again." I shrugged and pointed to the mess visible through the office doors. "I didn't go back in. Nothing has been touched since 7:45. Those are staff files, so please use some discretion."

Time seemed to stop as Nate snapped several pictures and dusted for fingerprints. He casually asked, "Are there any other cases you guys have been into recently? Big ones. Other than the Nichols case?"

"Well, there was the burglary of the electronics warehouse in the West

14

End. You guys tagged the Munson brothers for that. The case is due for sentencing next week. We were looking at shipping the older brother to the Detention Center for nine months. The younger one is headed for the Workhouse three-week program." I scrunched up my lips and thought for a second. Nate just waited.

"Then there is the Toivunen murder case." I looked at Nate and he gestured for me to go on. "Nate, do you think this is tied somehow to last night? That case is nowhere close to trial, and Nichols is in pretrial detention with no release privileges. Lou had him on probation when the murder occurred."

Nate was taking notes. I felt a strong pang of intuition about Lou's statement that Nichols was pulling strings from detention. "Hey, those staff files contain home addresses and phone numbers. Lou isn't scheduled to come in until two o'clock today. Maybe we should call him to make sure he's OK."

"You really think that's necessary?" He looked skeptical. "What are the chances this is about him?"

"Why are you here? You obviously thought it prudent to respond to this even with that murder on your plate."

For a brief moment, I wondered about the unknown person who dared to break into the offices of a criminal justice agency, and I knew it was someone I would have to take seriously. My intuitive voice was nagging at me not to let this go.

"I have his cell number programmed into my phone. It will just take a minute."

"Have at it," Nate agreed.

"No answer, but that isn't unusual. He isn't on call. Let me try his home phone." There was no answer there, either, but I left a message on his machine to call me on my cell phone right away. "Can you send a squad to his house?" I asked. "I'm sure I'm overreacting, but hey, it is better to be safe than sorry, right? Better yet, let's go there together; I know where it is."

"Let's hope you are overreacting, Jo. Kids love Lou. I've seen him get down off the witness stand after testifying against gang-bangers about their gang involvement, and he is still the first person they ask for when they're in trouble. Even if this is tied to Nichols, chances are Lou isn't a target. I just can't see it." He smiled a crooked little smile. "Let me radio this in. I don't want anyone thinking I'm just out socializing with you. That would be some gossip, wouldn't it?"

"You could do worse," I responded, thinking that Jerome Nathan knew just when to lighten my mood.

Chapter 3

LOU'S HOUSE SEEMED empty. It was 10:30 A.M., and he should have been up, even though I knew that he had probably been working quite late.

"Is it possible he got called to assist some of your guys.?" I asked Nate.

"Nothing going on that I'm aware of. Well, let's take a closer look. Stand back here. You guys really should be armed, you know."

"That's a different discussion, Nate." I started formulating an argument in my head about how probation officers must be part police officers, part counselors, and part social workers. We find it difficult to fulfill all of these roles while carrying guns, but the police usually don't understand that.

Two quick knocks and the door cracked open. Nate was all cop as he yelled into the residence. "Lou, you there? Lou, police!" Nothing. Nate motioned with his hand for me to wait. He entered with gun drawn. "It's all messed up here, too." Nate had his radio out immediately. "Squad 23 requesting backup at 1238 Pineview Court."

He stepped back out to wait for his backup. A Pathfinder pulled up in the drive, and Lou got out with a quizzical look on his face.

"Hey guys, what's up? Can't be a social call this time of morning."

"Where is your wife, Lou?" Nate asked quickly.

Lou took a step forward toward the doorway. Nate put a hand to his chest.

"Where's your wife?"

"Working. Now tell me what's going on," Lou demanded, looking worried.

"Your boss's office was broken into. Now it looks like your house got turned."

Two squads pulled up without sirens, and two uniformed officers quickly approached. Nate directed Lou and me to stay on the sidewalk while he entered the house with the two officers.

"All clear," Nate called out after five minutes or so.

"Lou, I need you to come in and do a quick visual of what's missing. Jo, you can stand in the entryway, but don't touch anything." Even though I approved of Nate's care in handling the crime scene, I fumed.

Lou flinched as he walked into the wreckage that was his living room. He visibly shrunk when he scanned the broken picture of his family. He just stood there and finally said in a quiet voice, "Nothing's missing that I can see right now. I have some guns in the basement—a couple of hunting rifles. I don't own any handguns."

"You guys drive me nuts. You should all carry!" Nate was about to start ranting again.

"Could you possibly make your point a little clearer, Nate?" I had to give him some grief.

"OK, let's go see about the guns."

Against orders, I followed the two men into the basement. The guns were still in a locked gun cabinet. Lou checked the utility area and his remodeled family room. He didn't notice anything out of place.

"Nice work, Lou, the place looks great," Nate said, trying for some normalcy in a day that had already become far from ordinary.

"Thanks, Sara picked out the wainscot and the carpet. I just muscled it into place." As he was looking around, he said, "I can't see anything out of order here. Let's go back upstairs."

On the way up the stairs, he was shaking his head. "I can't tell what they were looking for. I mean, it must be work related, right? With Jo's office being broken into and all." He paused at the landing, scratched his chin, and looked down at some imaginary spot in the carpeting.

"Let me see if I have this straight. Your theory is that they were looking for my address in Jo's office, tracked my house down, and then came here and tossed the place. Nothing is missing. It's just messed up. So, is this a message? To me? What's with all these messages to me?"

"We don't know yet," Nate responded.

We made our way back into the living room, and Nate began, "Your wife is at work, right?" Lou nodded with a shrug.

"Please don't misinterpret this question, but where were you just now?"

"I was at the gym."

"Do you go every day at this time?"

"Not really. My schedule is too irregular. I work three days, two off, five on, three off. Ten-hour shifts. We end up swapping shifts all the time."

"When you work until midnight, are you in the habit of going to the gym in the morning?" Nate persisted.

"Yes, why? What do you think it means?" Lou was clearly spooked.

"Nothing yet. I'm just trying to get as many pieces to this puzzle as I can. I'm going to have the Crime Scene Unit go through this place. Can you call Sara and tell her what happened so she doesn't walk into crime tape? They should be in and out of here in three hours."

"Sure." Lou pulled out his phone and hit speed dial.

"Let's go somewhere to talk about your caseload and who might have it in for you," Nate suggested.

"How about Ground Under?" I said. "It's six blocks away." Some of my staff members call the place my second office because I frequently meet them there for informal updates.

Lou gave me a knowing look and said, "See ya there, Jo."

Ground Under was full of its usual bustle. We descended the steps leading to the basement of the strip mall where it's located. The walls had a textured earthen tone, and the concrete floor had been stained to look like mud tiles, and then polyurethaned over. College kids and coffee junkies all huddled together in an aromatic, coffee-buzzed mass. I relaxed when I smelled my third cup brewing. I secretly longed to sit in the overstuffed chair and couch section, but it was not private enough. I resigned myself to be happy with my brew: strong, Ground Under java.

"So Lou, tell me who you've pissed off recently," Nate began.

"You mean kids, or professionals? We're OK, right Jo?" Lou was only half kidding. He has been known to offend people in high places by sometimes throwing out the rulebook.

Lou winked at me. I wondered to myself if he knew that he was good looking and was using it to his advantage. I found it curious that it worked on me. What did this guy have? I sat there thinking about my affection for Lou and wondered if somehow everyone knew he was my favorite. Then I let go of the guilt trip. Everybody loves Lou, men and women alike. The women like him because he brings hand-picked flowers for the clerical staff all summer long and is generally a good guy. If he forgets about the sign-out board, he apologizes by bringing a treat for everyone. The men like him because he is just an everyday guy. He does his share of after-work socializing, plays golf, and seems to genuinely care about everyone as his extended family. The kids he works with look to him as a father figure—even the hard-hearted gang kids. I think he just genuinely likes people, even the kids no one else likes. He is popular with the police because he shares information between our two agencies and because he knows so much about Duluth's community of troubled kids. I absolved myself of all guilt and tuned back into the conversation.

"Tell me about all of it. Whatever comes to your mind." Nate continued.

"Well, there's the Toivunen murder. Nichols is in lockup, though."

Lou and I exchanged a glance.

"Tell me about his gang ties. Is there a tie to you?" Nate grabbed his pen and poised it on his notepad. "Anything. Just talk."

I settled in and began sipping, as Lou is known both for his ability to talk and an amazing capacity for retaining even the smallest detail about his work.

"I first got Nichols after he committed a burglary when he was fifteen. This was after he came here from Detroit with his mom and little sister to escape gang life. There's not much to like about this kid, and I can find something to like about almost every kid." Lou shrugged, and Nate and I both nodded in response. "He enrolled at Central and hooked right up with the Gangster Mob. I actually think he is the leader. GM is a new gang with no apparent ties to other gangs.

"It's difficult to start a new gang, particularly in a city the size of Duluth. While the drug trade is still relatively small, it is growing. The market for drugs here is quite good. The price of a rock of crack is twice what a dealer can get in Minneapolis, Chicago, or Detroit. Breaking into such a lucrative market is tough and dangerous." Nate and I knew this, but we just let Lou continue to think out loud.

"Word has it, our friend Nichols has had quite a battle on his hands. For a guy to gain respect, he has to carve out his territory with pure violence." Lou paused to see if we fully grasped what he was saying. Again we nodded, not wanting to interrupt. "Any threats to the territory must be handled quickly and decisively. To gain access to a gang, one must be beaten or raped in." I could see the sadness settle into him from his first-hand experience in dealing with kids. "This is true for males and females. Nichols must have led the initiation of each and every new recruit. This is one tough kid. He is the kind of kid who doesn't feel anything except power. He also mistakes fear for respect. Legend has it he cut a kid's finger off and left it in the mailbox of his parents' house because the kid flashed an index finger gang sign. The members of the GM are terrified of Nichols. The GM has both juvenile and adult members, and he could easily be pulling strings from detention."

I sat there trying to figure out how this little weasel I had met with Lou was capable of a cold-blooded murder and running an entire gang. He seemed way too edgy to me. Way too out of control. I kept my thoughts to myself. I wondered if Lou remembered that I had gone with him to see Nichols in detention.

"We don't have that much information on this gang yet because they haven't been around that long. What the informants have said, though, is that Nichols is the kingpin. The leader. The leader usually makes sure that his runners and dealers don't use drugs. They need to keep it strictly professional. Nichols, however, thought he was above all of that. He thought he was hiding his use from everyone, but everyone knew. He started getting a god complex, too. Odds are he was losing touch with reality when he shot Toivunen. I'm bettin' that if he hadn't been doing the fast burn on meth, he would've had someone else carry out the hit on Toivunen. He got too cocky and careless." Lou took another sip of coffee, thought for a second, and went on.

"When he got picked up on the murder charge, the police needed time to investigate to make sure they charged him well. I'm holding him in detention on a violation of probation. The guy was really pissed off. Made a threat to me. He said, 'You will regret this. Don't you know who I am?' I didn't think that much of it. I mean, kids threaten me all the time. It is just bravado, trying to save face. Jo, remember? You were there. He threatened you, too. He asked, 'Is that your signature on my report? You're gonna pay, too.' Jo goes with us on all of our serious arrests and court hearings so she can watch our backs." Lou's expression had turned sober, free of his earlier mockery.

I thought to myself that I was just protecting my assets.

I asked Lou if he had been keeping a gang book.

"I'll make a short list for you of its known members, the colors, symbols, and our stab at the hierarchy. The problem is, I don't have that much yet. Some of the symbols have been borrowed or are slightly different from those used by other gangs like the Gangster Disciples, Latin Kings, Crips, and Bloods. This is going to be harder than you think."

"Lou," I cautioned him. "I'm not sure I want you anywhere near the office, let alone on the streets."

"I am not going to let this stop me. Think about the message we give to these guys if we back down. We need to come at them with everything we have."

"Nate, can you assign him an officer to team with for a while?"

"Sure, how about me?" Nate spoke up. "Let's go at this thing together, Lou."

"I'd like to be kept in the loop here whenever possible." My organizing skills kicked in. "I'd also like it if the same information packet you are preparing for the Police Department gets to the probation officers. Can we access the BCA database of known gang members and their ties to Detroit? Maybe he brought some of his buddies from there with him."

"I'm on it. We have access at the PD." Nate's enthusiasm was building.

"I'll be at the PD roll call for the first update," I continued. "Lou, please post the informational packet regionwide and have it distributed to all the mailboxes locally."

"Already there, boss."

"We can also check the Statewide Supervision System, Juv E Net, and Crim Net."

"There, too."

Nate offered to drop me at the office, continuing his diatribe about arming probation officers. I was thinking about the relative safety of Lou and anyone else who might be the target of this "warning" as well as how long it would take to clean up my office. Nate sensed my distraction, and we rode in silence for the last five minutes. As I exited the vehicle, he said, "We'll protect him, you know."

"Thanks, Nate. I know you will. Let's hope he doesn't need it."

* * * *

Chapter 4

THE DEPARTMENT was still in turmoil. Most of the staff had gathered in the reception area that houses three secretaries in a large open area divided by short cubicles. This arrangement works well because it allows maximum coverage at the front security window and the main phone line. I basked for a minute in the knowledge that these talented women would restore the atmosphere in our agency to that of an organized, fully functional office. The clerical staff not only handle large amounts of legal documents with ease but also manage to maintain an easygoing, friendly environment.

The secretaries are referred to as information specialists, but they essentially fill clerical positions. Staffed at a ratio of about one to every ten probation officers, they make the work readable and professional, and they enter information into the many legal databases. They are paid relatively well as clerical jobs go in the area, but they are still at the bottom of the pile relative to the other positions in the agency. They know that I know who really runs the place.

As I walked into my office, I was again stunned, but this time by the lack of disorder. My file cabinet was now closed with the drawer lip still bent. My plants looked to be healthy and reunited with their potting soil, and my desk was clean and organized. I turned to go back up front to investigate when I saw Jeannie walking toward me. I could tell that it was her even though the hallway is a good one-hundred feet long because her pink spiked hair was immediately discernable. She sports a different hairdo about every month that usually incorporates a bright dye job of pink, purple, or green. Her personality is at great odds with this rebellious presentation. She is bright, efficient, and professional. I waited while she traversed the distance. She approached with a guarded smile.

"I hope you don't mind, Jo, but I thought you could use some help."

"Thanks, Jeannie. You are truly the best."

As a supervisor, she had confidential privileges and could access the files without harm.

"I think I made some improvements in your filing system, but don't get used to me doing your filing."

"I'll keep searching for the right bribe, and again, thank you." I made a mental note to buy her favorite sugar-free box of chocolates from the gourmet chocolate store downtown. She had indeed improved my filing system for the staff files, and my desk contents were totally organized as well. I asked her to call building management to fix the lock, but she said it was already in the works. I went through the files, but found nothing missing.

I sent out a group e-mail to the juvenile unit staff regarding an emergency staff meeting at 2 P.M. I didn't think we would have an attendance problem and fully expected to see a couple of folks come in from vacation.

I called Chief Long and updated him in greater detail about the situation. He asked me to remind everyone on staff that he was the only person authorized to speak to the media. He also inquired about the effort to protect Lou. While Long knew about Lou's talent for reaching into the hearts of the hardened kids, he was also aware of his total lack of care for the chain of command and the bureaucratic rules of the office. Lou was known for bypassing the rules to accomplish his goals. He gave the classic "end justifies the means" excuse. Most of the time he was well connected enough to pull it off. A sizable income generated by an outside gang consulting business allowed him the freedom to take risks.

As expected, the staff and supervisors were on board about finding the culprits. This group really mobilized in difficult situations. It reminded me of a time a while back when one of the probation officers in the adult felony unit was having his house vandalized on a daily basis. A brick was thrown through his large living room picture window while his wife and two sons were home. Two of his cars were also sabotaged, and his insurance company was about to drop him. We set up a six-block radius of personnel staked out in cars, on foot, and hiding in bushes. The Police Department was notified and had squads in the area ready to respond. When a car approached his house, we let the bad guy get out of his vehicle and partway to the house before moving in.

He made it back to his car, and a high-speed chase ended a few blocks away in a police roadblock. That put an end to the PO's problems.

After the 6:10 P.M. PD roll call, I swung by Lou's house to make sure it was under obvious surveillance and made my way back home. I took the scenic route that winds along the shores of Lake Superior. I was cautious, as the deer were everywhere. They cross two highways to get to Lake Superior water. Poor things, they always remind me of my dogs. I can't get over how desensitized we have all become in this town to the ritual of deer killing. The news programs regularly show images of hunters stringing up their kill and cutting the heads off right on camera. I'm sure they feel they are portraying the correct way to prepare the deer for Chronic Wasting Disease testing, but I gag every time. What is this doing to our children? No wonder I have so much job security.

I put a blues tape in the CD player and tried to relax in my 1985 Range Rover. Were it not for the paint job, it would be hard to tell her age because of the timeless boxy body style and prominent roof rack that have remained steady in the Range Rover for nearly twenty years. It was red at one time, but sun-fade damage had rendered it a pale pink. I bought it in Arizona after my dad spent the better part of a winter searching for it. It had high miles but a rust-free body and leather interior. I drove it home and promptly brought it to my mechanic, Phil.

He is wiry with a ready smile and an appetite for intelligent conversation. He has a slightly curly beard, perpetually greasy hands, and eyes that are so light blue, they appear white if his face is particularly dirty. His shop is a block from my office, and he caters to all of the civil servants who work nearby. Phil sent the motor out to have the cylinder heads bored-out, and he rebuilt the rest of it in his shop. He replaced the struts, most of the front end, and the tires. I then took it to the electronic store to have a six-speaker stereo system installed. The beauty of this vehicle is that I have no car payment. It is reliable as hell and ugly enough so that it is not a target for thieves. My work has left me a little jaded about crime.

By the time I got home, it was 7:30. I let the dogs out and allowed them to sniff my clothes so that they could determine my activities for the day. When we hit the trail, it was dark, with the moon at three-quarters full so I didn't need a headlamp. I marveled about how different the woods looked day to night, and season to season. The temperature had dropped below freezing, and the smell was danker than decomposing leaves. The moon lighted the trail so well I could make out mushrooms that looked like little fiddle heads in clumps along the trail. I predicted that the fiddle heads would be gone in three days if the temps kept dropping.

Inside, I started a fire, nuked some leftover lasagna, and parked in front of the TV. Sadly, I found myself watching FBI Files on a satellite channel. I should broaden my focus.

I called Lou on his cell at 10 P.M. He was working the intensive program with his usual partner, Amanda. Intensive probation means daily contact with the offenders in their homes, as well as tracking their movements twenty-four hours a day. Nate, who was riding along, did not get introduced at every house and was mistaken for an intern twice. That gave us all a chuckle. There must be some pretty old students in college these days. There was nothing out of the ordinary going on, and it was business as usual in the intensive probation unit. Nate and Lou would soon be able to focus entirely on the gang issue, and if or how it tied to the Nichols/Toivunen murder. They had twenty kids on the caseload, were planning on seeing twelve that night, with a double check on two of them. Nate was having one heck of a long day. I smiled inwardly at his dedication to protecting Lou. I also smiled at Lou's insistence on finishing out his intensive duties before transferring out temporarily. I felt a little guilty because I knew I had the weekend ahead of me, but Lou had to work.

I cleaned my solitary dish and took a moment to appreciate the order and comfort of living alone. There were no dirty dishes in the sink, no clutter of art projects to work around. No dead or dying vegetables in the fridge. I did two average loads of laundry a week. It was all nice and predictable. Would I get bored with this? Had I become too rigid to live with someone again? Was it worth it?

Cocoa and Java allowed me to settle into bed first before sandwiching me in. They both tend to cuddle closer and closer throughout the night. I suspect all three of us snore softly. I basked in the simple pleasures of dog love. It was predictable, loyal, and most of all, unconditional.

Chapter 5

Saturday morning, we set off through freshly fallen snow. The trail looked, smelled, and felt totally different for the third day in a row. The fiddle-top mushrooms were covered and invisible. The "boys" were like kids in their first snowfall—wrestling and rolling in the snow at every turn. I always savor my first snowy walk of the season. But on this day, I wasn't quite satisfied with the new blanket of whiteness. I wished for a snow big enough to require snowshoes.

As soon as we neared the house, the dogs slowed, and the hair came up on Cocoa's back. She let out a guttural growl usually reserved for bears. I flashed on the staff files and remembered that my address had been on my pay stub in the top drawer of my desk. I grabbed both dogs and walked them over to my neighbor Carol's place. Her property and mine are connected by a trail that we both mow to a halfway point. To avoid leaving visible tracks from my place to hers, I backtracked and took a longer path that comes out on our connecting trail three hundred yards east of my property line. I told her I thought someone had broken into my house and asked her if I could leave the dogs with her for a little bit so that I could investigate. She agreed. Cocoa and Java headed straight for the treat jar. They sat perfectly mannered, side by side, just staring at it. I apologized to her, and she laughed, walked over to the jar, and took out a treat for each of them.

Carol is known as the dog lady. She regularly dog-sits for her friends, and the mutts absolutely adore her. She has an endless supply of treats, takes the dogs on many, many walks, and loves their little tails off. Carol is perpetually single, but no one really knows why. She is attractive, fit, creative, and personable. She has sandy blond hair, blue eyes, and a warm smile. Her friends have tried to set her up with dates, but she seems perfectly content with her dogs and her books.

I left my canines in Carol's capable hands, and rather than taking the trail, walked down her driveway to the road, then cut over to the front of my property. There was an older jacked-up Blazer on the shoulder. Footprints led toward my house through the woods. I found the vehicle unlocked, and popping the hood, quickly pulled two spark plug wires. I eased the hood down and considered my next move. My house is one hundred yards in from the road. My driveway has a gentle curve so that cars passing by can't see the house. The guy I hired to put it in had a difficult time visualizing it, or understanding why I would want it that way, since it would cost more. Once it was done, he understood the visual appeal as well as the practicality of it.

I decided to take a different route to get closer to the house. I called 911 on my cell phone, telling the dispatcher about my plight. I specifically asked her to call the Duluth Police Department after informing the township police. I gave the 911 operator a quick rundown on the forty-eight hours leading up to the intrusion. The township guy, Dan Shilhon, would be here quickly, but I knew he would want backup. The township PD's home base was in the town hall located a mile away on Valley Road. Dan was either on duty there or at his home a mile in the other direction. Either way, it was going to be quick. I decided to hunker down in view of the vehicle, resisting the urge to see if the shithead was torching my place.

The wait seemed endless. Although I see myself as a minimalist, I really love my house. I think anyone who has built their own house board by board would have been hard-pressed to sit outside and wait for help while an intruder did god knows what to it. I was mortified that all of my work could go up in smoke. I quickly amended that thought. It would be our work that would go up in smoke. A major contributor to building my house was my best friend and neighbor, Kathy, who is a designer/architect. She designed the post and beam house I call my home. It is a simple one-story building with exposed ash beams. The living room, dining room, and kitchen all flow into one another. I have a Russian woodstove in the living room area that is made of native Lake Superior rock. The floors are all maple, with an in-floor, water-circulated heating system built in. It has a huge master bedroom with a gas fireplace, and a Jacuzzi. Kathy insisted that I install a solar panel to power the water system. She calculated that it would pay for itself in ten years of energy cost savings.

The shower has three showerheads. All told, my home cost about what an old house in the area would go for. It took Kathy and me two years to build it, and I have been enjoying living in it for the past five years. Now I help Kathy with all of her home-repair projects. I think I could help her for a lifetime and not pay her back for all of the work she put into my house. She doesn't keep track of who owes whom. In fact, we always joke about owing each other. We both enjoy creating something and just hanging out together.

Kathy is one of the most casual and laid back people I know. She wears pants fortified with homemade patches and twenty-year-old jackets held together with duct tape. She is not at all like the first impression she gives. Her clothing is at great odds with the beauty and sensitivity of her designs, and her hands can build anything. Her house is incredible. I have often wondered if all of the building Kathy has done has contributed to her wide shoulders, or if it was genetics that led her toward her trade. She has medium length curly brown hair, graying in streaks around her face, and eyes the color of chestnuts. She lives with her partner, Donna, a major fem who has never picked up a hammer in her life.

I waited five eternal minutes, visualizing every square inch of my house, trying to avoid thinking about what might be happening in there, until I couldn't stand it any longer. I headed toward the house. The nearest trees were mostly assorted pines about sixteen years old and provided little cover, so I moved slowly. When I was in view of the house, I stopped, slowed my breathing, and listened. It was nearly dark now, and I could barely make out footprints, but I could see tracks leading to the rear entrance. I slowly, painstakingly, made my way around back. I'm sure the intruder was expecting the dogs and me to come crashing out of the woods. I could see that tracks were definitely leading into the house, and I was immediately pissed off.

My anger was instantly cooled by remembering the four—no, five— dead Toivunens. What the hell were they trying to pull? Did they think we would get so scared we would just let Nichols out? I flashed on Nichols's threat to Lou and me while we served him his violation papers to hold him for murder charges. The arrogant shit probably thought that if he scared me, I'd just arrange for his accidental release. Perhaps this was just a vendetta. I decided I wanted to see who I was dealing with, so I threw a rock out near the front of the house where I have two motion sensitive lights. Both of them flooded the front area with light. I could see some movement in the house, and a head popped up near the front window that overlooks the driveway. I could tell he was male, but there was no way to tell if he was armed. He was obviously lying in wait.

I heard a car coming up the drive. Hoping it was more than one, I waited. Two squads rolled to a stop and parked nose to nose blocking the driveway but pointing at a 45-degree angle to the house. Headlights were on, but there were no flashing lights. The township officer and two Duluth Police officers exited the vehicles. Two of them approached the house, staying as close to the building as possible, while one covered the back door. Suddenly, I heard a huge crash and knew the intruder had broken the window overlooking the deck on the south side of my house. He jumped the rail and bounded off into the woods just as the officer rounded the corner.

"Freeze, police."

The intruder fired two shots over his shoulder as he ran off into the denser woods south of my house. Two of the officers gave chase, firing shots of their own. The township cop, Shilhon, stayed behind. I stood up and walked over to him. He had his gun out, and I swear, nearly shot me.

"Dan, Dan, it's me, Jo. I called you." My voice was an octave higher than usual.

"Shit, Jo! Where were you?"

"I was watching from the woods. I sabotaged his car. He has to be headed that way."

"Duluth Township Police to squad 24. Suspect is likely headed to the vehicle on Valley Road. The home owner rendered it undriveable. She is with me and safe." Then he turned his attention back to me, showing little of the relief he must have felt about not shooting his friend and neighbor. "Jo, sorry about that. Come with me to the squad."

We both jumped in and quickly drove to the end of the drive. I was ordered to "Stay." I did. The intruder had outrun the police in enough time to try the car and run up Valley Road.

The two DPD officers, Hannon and Striker, radioed dispatch the status of "subject" and called all available squads to the area. The Sheriff's Department provides backup to the township police in all of the outlying areas. All told, there were five squads responding.

"Subject has fled on foot and may be trying to steal a vehicle." Striker's voice reported into the radio.

The area is accessible by only two roads. The main highway is two miles away. Officers blocked the access roads, and Dan went door to door warning people of the danger and asking them to remove the keys from any vehicles on their property. Residents of this area regularly leave keys in their cars. I suspected that this would change all that. A half mile up the road, Dan discovered that a home owner's four-wheeler had been stolen from his barn.

After hearing this, I walked up the driveway to my house to brew a fresh pot of French roast. I boiled a pot of water on the stove and got out my French press. I needed the ritual of preparing it, and I craved the heightened aroma of this type of preparation. I avoided looking at the footprints scattered in front of every window of my house. I was pissed as hell about the invasion. I also realized that he had been there, in my house, with a gun, waiting for me. I called my neighbor Carol and updated her, thanking her profusely. She would keep the pups as long as necessary.

Dan tracked me back to my house, and we sipped coffee at the breakfast bar. Dan is a marathon runner and has a lean, intelligent look. He also has classic Finnish features along with the requisite Finnish stoicism. I bet he plays a great game of poker. I invited him to use my house as a gathering place. He declined, as the township station was close by.

The phone rang just as I was seeing Dan out the door. It was Nate calling to see if I had another place to stay. They were going to have a difficult time surveilling both my house and Lou's, since I did not live in the jurisdiction of the DPD, and the Sheriff's Department didn't have that kind of manpower. I told him I had a place. Then I asked, "Have you identified my intruder?"

"Well, the plates from the Blazer came back stolen. We've tracked it to Detroit. There is a good chance our guy is part of the Gangster Mob. No way to tell if it's the same person responsible for the Toivunens. Whoever he is, there's a good chance he's in some big trouble for screwing up this hit, if it was supposed to be a hit."

That comforted me a lot.

I put duct tape and cardboard over my broken window, packed clothes and dog food, picked up the boys at Carol's, and went to Kathy's. The dogs seemed a little bummed to leave but were always up for a ride in the car. I let them run in front of the car for the last two-mile stretch of dirt road leading to Kathy and Donna's house.

I had not called first, and Kathy and Donna just opened up the door when they saw my bag and two dogs. They were about to sit down to a midday dinner of chicken, baked potatoes, and salad, and they set another plate. I slowly filled them in, leaving out any names. They stopped eating and stared in silence. When she finally spoke, Kathy said, "Holy shit, Jo, you have to get another job. Now."

That made me laugh a little.

"I'm not kidding, Jo, this is your life. It's not worth it."

Donna was crying. I hate that. I just can't stand watching someone cry.

I stiffened. "That isn't going to happen. I love my job. It isn't like this. I'm a desk jockey. I have very little direct client contact. I just run the unit. The folks I work with are awesome." It occurred to me that I was sounding defensive and trying to fast-talk myself out of their disapproval, but I kept on. "Their job is to connect with kids, help them turn their lives around, and protect the public. This is very unusual."

They just stared at me, incredulous. They didn't kick me out, though. I really needed the sleep, and I was secretly scared shitless. That guy could have been there for one of several reasons: to kill me, or my dogs, or to simply deliver a message. I realized that I may never know which.

I felt safe in the comfort of my friends' guest bed. They both snored lightly, and that comforted me, too.

Chapter 6

THE REST OF THE weekend proved to be uneventful. I kept checking my cell phone because I couldn't believe Lou had not called.

Monday morning over coffee, Kathy told me not to worry about my dogs. She works out of her home, and they can run free at her house all day. Kathy and Donna own a large spread, and their house is three hundred yards from the nearest dirt road and another two miles from Valley Road. They also have two dogs, a cat, and a goat. My boys have spent many days roaming their property while Kathy and I have done home improvement projects, stacked wood, or just hung out.

As I sat there sipping coffee, I was moved by how many times Kathy and Donna have been there for me—through the chaos of building my house, as well as my last two breakups. I have spent innumerable nights curled up with the two of them and all of the animals (except the goat) watching movies in their home entertainment room.

Kathy's parting words to me as I got into my Rover were, "Live your priorities, Jo."

I felt strong conflict between the comfort and love of my friends, their desire for my safety, and a responsibility to help get this gang eradicated from our city. I also had a sense of responsibility for Lou and the Toivunen family. I think I originally got into this business because I have justice issues. I want things to be fair and am known for my attempts at fairness with staff. I felt a strong tug in my heart to try and make this thing right. I also struggled, as Lou often did, with how much I could be involved. This was really the responsibility of the police. Our role was to bring them information about the kids we know and supervise in the community.

I resolved to do that from the safety of my desk.

Rolling into the parking lot, I noticed that many of the hunters had returned. The lot was nearly full. As I walked through the door, I realized that the staff had heard about my intruder. Since people were anxious to hear about what had happened, I held an impromptu staff meeting to capture some of their energy and try to channel it toward a solution. I went through the entire case history, beginning with the triangle of love between Nichols, Felicia Green, and Toivunen; the break-in at my office; Lou's break-in; the murder of the Toivunens; and finally, my intruder. We all reviewed the gang information list.

The PO's were first stunned, and then angry. Most vowed to help in any way possible. Don, one of the juvenile PO's who covered the office in my absence, immediately spoke up.

"Jo, we'll go to the schools today. We can get the informational packet out to all of the assistant principals." Because of the budget crisis, we no longer had Police Liaison Officers in the high schools. "We can also get it out to detention and the treatment facilities," he promised. "We'll put pressure on any known gang members in the area. I suspect this gang has no real rivals, but we can hope that some of the smaller gangs will give up information to try and gain back some of their territory."

"Thanks, guys. Go to it. Keep court covered, and keep me informed."

Warren, the PO who had volunteered to fill in for Lou with the intensive unit, was absent from the impromptu briefing. I walked down to his office to see what was up. He was on the phone with an irate parent, trying patiently to suggest that she actually try to parent her child and set some limits before calling him because "Ricky wouldn't do the dishes." He just shook his head at me with raised eyebrows and said that he would be happy to give her his supervisor's number if she preferred, but that he couldn't and wouldn't intervene until she had at least tried to do what he had suggested as an intervention. I shook my head back at him, waved, and backed out of his doorway. I was glad to see that Warren was busy with his caseload, even though retirement was just around the corner for him. I wanted to keep him engaged during his remaining couple of years.

I went back to my office and found a message to call Nate. When I reached him, he told me that the Blazer they had impounded from my house had prints all over it. They ran them and found the suspect's match in AFIS, the federal system for tracking adult felons' fingerprints. I guess he wasn't such a "little" bugger after all.

"His name is Donnie Nichols, a.k.a. Smithy, a.k.a. Gunner. He got his nicknames from his love of guns. He is also the big brother to our very own Mike Nichols. Detroit, as you know, is infamous for having poor Bureau of Criminal Apprehension records and fingerprinting due to a seriously overloaded system. When you call there looking for information, it is rare to ever get a call back." Nate continued. "Your buddy Lou came through with this information because of a training contact there, a jewel in the rough who did some digging. The guy gave us a lot of information." I could picture Nate turning his hands palms up, and nodding as he spoke into the phone.

"It turns out Donnie and Mike Nichols are half brothers. They have the same dad but different moms. Dad is in prison for armed robbery and goes by the name of Bull." He paused, and I could hear him shuffling his notes. He wasn't quite as good at this as Lou. Lou would have easily committed all of the facts to memory. "Bull was raised in the Detroit projects and worked his way up to lieutenant in the Ram gang. He went to prison for an armed robbery charge and will be eligible for parole in three years. His two boys were raised separately but hooked up with Bull by visiting him in prison. Together, they began a pretty successful drug-running operation in Duluth this year by collaborating with the Native Mob. Then they decided to make Duluth their own and created a new gang, borrowing heavily from the structure of the Mob, the Latin Kings, and their father's gang. They're suspected of several assaults and two robberies. The two boys are thick as thieves and run with a group of four other known gangsters: Spade, Little Moe, Ice, and Mice. Isn't that cute? Ice and Mice are also brothers. Our Detroit contact is working on their real names. The Detroit gang task force list of suspected and known gang members is huge."

The police certainly had been busy. "Well, the brother connection is big. Are you close to locating him? Smity, or Smithy? Whatever the hell his name is. Big Nichols."

"We have an all-squads bulletin out from here to Detroit. What's so hard about this is that they are so new to town. With the viciousness of their attacks, the usual informants on the street aren't talking. The Gangster Mob is predominantly Caucasian, so its members can easily hide in a town the size of Duluth. We did get a description from the BCA of the older Nichols boy's tattoos, though, and he is covered with symbols from his old gang, mostly skulls, guns, and ammo. He could have altered them, but usually that means turning them into something similar. For example, I've seen a knife turned into a snake. The symbols will still usually be recognizable in their new form. The packet Lou sent out has possible symbols in it, so we are still on track with that. Every officer from here to Detroit should be checking tattoos and colors. Maybe Smithy will get tagged for speeding." He took a breath and seemed to calm down a bit, so I changed the subject.

"What is the status of Mike Nichols? Has he been moved to the jail yet?"

"Absolutely. He's in isolation, and he isn't talking. Well, actually, he did say one thing. This guy has some ego. He said, 'There are more of us than you know, and you can't stop us.'"

"Do you think he's bluffing?"

"I don't know. Lou doesn't think so."

"How is Lou holding up?"

"Fine. I'd like to steal him, you know."

"He won't even think about it. He'll be eligible for a full pension in a few more years with us, and then I suspect you will have to pay through the nose for his services."

"I suppose you're right. How are you holding up, Jo? Sorry about your house."

"I'm fine. Kind of pissed off about it. I miss my house. I also don't want my life ruined by these punks. I have great friends and a safe place to stay. Do you think it would be safe for me to move back in yet?"

"Hard to say. I don't know if this was supposed to be a hit or a warning. You could install a security system."

"I've contemplated that, but they could still get to my dogs. I couldn't bear that. I'm pretty sure they know the dogs exist now."

"Well, I wouldn't risk it, Jo. This can't go on forever. We'll get 'em. Let me know if there's anything I can do."

"Thanks."

As soon as I hung up, the phone rang. "Jo Spence," I answered.

"Josephine?"

"Hi Dad." Only my father uses my given name. About three years ago, he called the front desk looking for me and asked for Josephine. They told him no one by that name worked there. I had to reassure him that I still had a job and that I'm known as Jo. Parents.

"What's up, Dad?"

My dad remarried quickly after my mom died five years ago. He lives in Duluth during the summer and Arizona during the winter. He regularly reads the Duluth newspaper on-line from Arizona in the winter. He and his new wife had driven down there in October.

"I read an interesting story in the paper this morning." He added accusingly, "Are you OK?"

"What did it say, Dad? I haven't read it yet."

"It said you nearly got killed by gangsters. Obviously you aren't dead; now tell me what's going on!"

"Well, as you probably read, there is a big case here, and we're working on it with the police. Some kids were just trying to send me a message. I was in no real danger. Message received. I'm not front line on this." I was sounding defensive for the second time in a matter of hours. "I'm not staying at home right now. I'm safe."

"Are you sure? You are welcome here any time. We can go fishing. Whatever."

"I may just take you up on that, but really, it's OK. How about I call you more often for a while so you can stop worrying?"

"That would be great. Thanks, honey."

"Here is my cell number. Call it anytime, too. OK?"

"OK, I'll probably lose it, but go ahead... Got it. We love you."

"I love you both, too. Give Lois a hug for me."

I sat there staring out the window that looks out over Lake Superior, thinking about my 82-year-old father. He stands six feet and weighs 180 pounds, and he has a full head of white hair that he keeps closely cropped. He is in great shape from ballroom dancing and playing softball in the over-80 league three nights a week. He is, however, losing his short-term memory, and I was glad he had met Lois right after my mom died. She is a great woman who loves him as he deserves, but she also can put him in his place when he needs it. I love her for that. I pictured them playing cards every morning to see who gets to be boss for the day.

My mom had that same spunk. I allowed myself to miss her for a minute. I was the youngest of five, and the only girl, and my mom used to refer to me as "her baby girl." This did set me up a bit with my siblings, so I had to learn how to fight, or run fast. My mom used to spoil me rotten. She had waited so long for a girl. The problem was, I was a tomboy. She had to find it in her heart to forgive me that transgression, and to let go of her dreams of white dresses, pink hats, and the like when I hit five and began kindergarten. I hated dresses. How could I play baseball, tag, or anything fun in a dress and little black shoes? For the first week of school, my mom sent me off in a dress. By day two, I was packing a bag of jeans, tennis shoes, and a T-shirt to change into on the way to school. I don't know how she found out, but she let me dress myself after that first week. Perhaps she resigned herself to getting only five years of pretty. She never stopped calling me her baby girl, or loving me absolutely. I really did miss her.

That got me thinking about the crush I had on my kindergarten teacher, Mrs. Smyth. I didn't recognize it as such then, but I totally adored her. I would sit in the front row and just smile up at her. Then there was a student aide who helped out in first grade, etc., etc., etc. I theorized that some people are born gay, and some people have romantic feelings for both genders. I have always felt gay. I am totally clear about that. I remembered that mom hadn't figured it out until I told her. She was shocked, but you guessed it, supportive.

Some of my friends were not so lucky. My dad, bless his still living soul, had me figured out long before I did. He asked me about my special friend once when I was about fifteen. I looked at him quizzically, and he let it go. He is an interesting man. He says some outright racist things. I think he was influenced in the navy during World War II somehow, but he is totally open in many other ways. He sometimes catches himself in his oppressive thoughts and works it out right in front of me. I give him points for trying.

I can't help thinking about softball when I think about the time in my life when I was figuring out who I was. I went to college locally just so I could play softball. I had the honor of watching several teammates come out, or be outed, to parents. Some of them were disowned, some merely shamed, and others referred to therapists. I was very lucky in the parents' lottery.

Reminiscing about my supportive family brought on that too familiar pang of sadness about my brother Mark, who is not so supportive. We were closest in age, at fourteen months apart. We had a significant sibling rivalry going on all through high school, and our separate groups of friends sometimes overlapped. He played football and mostly hung out with guys from the team. I played basketball and softball, and a large number of my teammates dated his teammates. We ended up at some of the same parties. He wasn't thrilled. He did not want me to know what he was up to. He portrayed a "good boy" image with mom and dad at home, and a "bad boy" image at school.

During his senior and my sophomore year, he got too drunk at a big party on the East End and I had to cover his ass with mom and dad. When I got home, I wrote my parents a note informing them that Mark had had to take care of one of his friends who had been in a skating accident, and he had taken him to the hospital. He would be home as soon as he could and didn't want them to worry. We were on better terms after that, but I think he always felt like I had something to use on him. I never would have. When I came out to him, he just ignored me. I sensed he took some sick pleasure in being the more "normal kid," whatever that means. By now, the guy was forty-two years old! Maybe he would always be just a homophobe. I vowed to ask him about it someday.

Chapter 7

I CALLED the local hardware store in Lakeside, inquiring about getting my window fixed. They couldn't come out to my home but gave me the name of a handyman who could. If he couldn't fix it on site, he would bring the whole window in. His name was Buddy Hinz. Why are most handymen named Buddy or Guy? Anyway, he would be out later that day to fix or remove it.

For most of the afternoon, I worked on staff evaluations. My only interruption was about a possible lead in the case. Lou called to let me know that Don had questioned one of his probationers who had been in detention with Nichols. Don suspected that Nichols had bragged up his status while in there. Sure enough, he had.

JT, a.k.a. Jimmy Tomlinson, had been in the same wing as Nichols. Nichols allegedly punched him while they were the only two in the shower, calling him a pretty girl. This happened away from the guards, but they knew something had happened.

JT wouldn't talk about that but did tell Don that Nichols was known to his gangsta' buddies as "Nickel." He went on to imitate Nichols. "Nickel cause I always got five grand on me. Easy money for me. I'm gonna run the police, take a legitimate business, and make a small mint out of running drugs in Duluth." He had big plans. Said he would be "outta here soon, just you wait and see. They gonna open those doors right up for me. Have a limmo right out front." JT also said that Nickel was up one minute, thinking he was god or something, then down the next.

"Weird," continued Lou. "But here is the good stuff. From what JT told him, Don thinks the Gangster Mob has been working out of an abandoned warehouse in the old steel mill complex in Morgan Park. The

41

closest neighborhood is six blocks away, and there is a gate. If this is the place, it will be an easy raid."

"When is it happening?"

"Four o'clock. Do you want to come?" I thought about Kathy and my Dad.

"No, I'll just get in the way. Have fun, and stay safe. Don't make me break my word to the Chief, OK?"

"No problem, boss."

"So, when do you call me Jo, and when am I boss?"

"Sorry, boss."

"How are things at home?" I hoped to elicit thoughts of his loved ones in his mind. "You don't have to do this, you know."

"Yes, I do."

"Call me if you need anything."

"Same for you."

The hardest part about being the boss is standing back and letting others do what they are supposed to do. Man, I wanted to get in there. I called Kathy and Donna to see if I could pick up takeout, and they took me up on the offer. The only bummer about living on the edge of town was being out of delivery range. No pizza delivery, no Cantonese, no Chinese, etc. I picked up takeout pizza for us and for the surveillance team at Lou's. That was a big hit. I also swung by my house to inspect the window situation. Buddy had taken the entire window out and boarded up the opening. It felt good to have that under way. I also took time to wipe up the footprints throughout my house. Soon things would be back to normal. Soon we would have our city back. I felt a pang of guilt for bringing such slime into the Valley. I was pissed off all over again. There were no signs of additional violation in my neighborhood or house. I hoped the raid was going well.

My cell phone rang just as I walked into Kathy and Donna's. I checked the caller I.D., put the pizza box on the table, and took the call in the bathroom.

"Jo, it's Lou. Here's the scoop. We got in and found one guy guarding the place with a machine gun. He opened fire, so the cops had to return it. The kid is dead. He was only fifteen or sixteen years old. We don't have an I.D. yet. We found an arsenal of guns, including some automatics, and a truckload of crack, powder cocaine, and pot. Huge amounts. The cops are still going through it. It looks to me like they received shipments here in moving vans, and this is the distribution center. It doesn't look like anyone but the guard lives here. There is a pool table, a video room filled with porn, action flicks, and some home videos of the gang. That's what I'm going to focus on. I'm taking the tapes back to the Police Department. We'll digitize them, blow up the pictures, and work on I.D.s. Hopefully, the search of this place will turn up an address. The police are a little maxed out about all the drugs. This is the biggest bust in the Midwest. They're having trouble focusing on anything else. I'll call you when I know anything more."

"Lou, tell me where you were when the raid happened."

"In the car, boss."

"Really?"

"Really!"

"Thanks."

"It was for you."

"And your family."

"Good point."

"Get some sleep tonight."

"Yes, boss."

By the time I hung up, dinner was on the table.

"So, how was work today, Jo?" Kathy's question sounded a tad dubious to me.

"Funny! We're making progress. Big drug bust today. You'll hear about it on the news. Don't worry, I was nowhere near it. In fact, it went down while I was on the way home. I made a conscious decision not to go." I hated how defensive I sounded. I felt like I was seven again.

"Excellent! We are proud of you."

I rolled my eyes and thought, *This must be how Lou feels*. While it was nice to be cared about, I couldn't really talk to them about this. *Shit!* I changed the subject.

"I arranged to get my window fixed today. Fields Hardware gave me the name of a guy. Should be fixed tomorrow or the next day."

"Great!"

"I also talked to my dad. He read about the intruder at my house in the newspaper. I can't believe they used my name. I don't need that."

"Why? Do you think it will mean more trouble?"

"I hadn't thought about that. Did you see the coverage? Did they give my address?"

"They didn't, just that you live in the Valley, and they gave your job title."

"Well, at least that part is good. I just don't like my work and home mixing. I don't want people worrying."

"Speaking of that, Dar called here today looking for you. I told her you were fine and that you were staying with us for now. Her number is on the phone board."

"Oh, great, how did she sound?"

"Concerned." I did not want to have to deal with Dar at all right then.

"Kathy, do you have headlamps? I could really use a walk. I'll take all of the pups."

"In the front hall, help yourself. The batteries are fresh in all of them, so you shouldn't need a backup. Mind if I go along?"

"Cool. Let's go."

We walked up the old railroad grade to the river and back in near silence. That was one thing I really loved about our friendship, her ability to share comfortable silences. It was a great trait to have in a friend. She did ask me if I was ready to begin dating yet. I told her I didn't know. I hadn't really done the closure thing with Dar, even though I was glad it was over. I didn't ask why she was asking.

Besides the grade, Kathy and Donna have a circular trail that connects to the west branch of the Little Knife River; the same river that borders my land and trail. The ski down the river from my house to theirs is incredible every time. It is especially incredible right after a heavy snowfall. The river is narrow and curving. There are sinewy cedar trees growing through dark shale rocks, pine trees of every variety, a few birch, and poplar trees. Heavy snow on the branches causes them to hang over the river. The effect is spectacular. My favorite time to ski or snowshoe is after dark, with a moon bright enough to navigate by. At the end of most skis, we have a hot sauna and run around naked in the snow until we are ready to heat up again. I couldn't wait for more snow. The snowfall we got the previous night was barely enough to cover the ground. Just a tease.

When we got back to the house, I called Dar. She had been worried after hearing about the intruder at my house and the likely attempted murder of Juvenile Probation Supervisor Jo Spence. I told her the story had been exaggerated. There had been an intruder, but the dogs had alerted me, and the police chased him off. I did not tell her about the gun or my little rock-throwing idea. We made a date to go to lunch the following day at the Lift Bridge Café. I could not tell how she was feeling about "us." If lunch didn't go well, I would still have a good view of the lake.

I couldn't find a comfortable spot in the unfamiliar bed and didn't sleep well. When I did fall asleep, I dreamed that someone else was living in my house. I drove up to come home, and there was a minivan in my garage. Inside, I could see someone washing dishes. I didn't know what to do about it. I just stood there. The stranger began looking out the window, and I ran and woke up.

In the next dream, I woke up happy to have a dog at my side, only to realize that it was a man. The man yelled, "Get out of my house! Get out of here!" Once again, I ran and woke up.

I tried one more time to sleep. I was standing in front of my coffeemaker about to pour a cup of French roast. The entire floor began to turn like a treadmill. I ran faster and faster, and all I could think was, "Damn, can't I get a fucking cup of coffee?" I woke up sweating. I finally gave up at 4:30 A.M., showered in the basement, made a pot of coffee, and began a note for Kathy and Donna. Before I had finished, Donna came down the stairs.

"Are you OK?"

"I couldn't sleep. It's not the bed or your place or anything. I think I'm just stressed out. I need to get a security system or something. Thanks, though."

She just walked over and gave me a hug, looked me in the eyes, and hugged me again. I thought about how lucky I was to have her in my life. She is secure enough to respect the friendship between Kathy and me, and also to be there for me herself. Amazing. She is such a fem too. That morning she was wearing her tiny white house robe with lavender fuzz around the collar.

With Kathy and me, the rules are simple. I help her with stuff; she helps me with stuff. We talk to each other about our relationships. We kick each other in the butt once in a while when the other is being a selfish jerk, or when we see the other giving up too much. Donna knows that Kathy talks to me about her. She doesn't try to be my best friend, or to put me in the middle. I know she is glad Kathy has me. I found myself wondering if I give Donna half as much as she gives to me. I wished that she could have a close friend, too. I knew of no one.

Chapter 8

MY CELL RANG on the way to work. I pulled over because there were too many dead spots along the way to permit an uninterrupted conversation. Nate filled me in on the activities of the Gangster Mob from the previous night.

He said that the surveillance van in front of Lou's had been shot to hell. They used it for drive-by target practice at 3 A.M. "Thank god, it was bulletproof. The guys inside didn't get off a shot. The good news is they didn't get shot, either. They couldn't pursue the shooters, though, because the engine compartment was not bulletproof. Suspects then evidently drove from Lou's to the Detention Center. It looked like they tried to shoot their way in, but they didn't make it.

The police found some blood near the entry doors, and they thought that the gang members shot at the bulletproof glass straight on, got hit by a ricochet, and gave up. The place was swarming with squads in under three minutes, but they were gone. They must have thought that Nichols was still in there. Even if they had penetrated the first door, the second door would have taken time. There is no way they would have had time to break anyone out. It took some guts to try, though. For sure, it took stupidity. Add a kid brain on drugs to firepower and money, and you have a very dangerous situation.

Nate relayed Lou's thoughts on the utter unpredictability of this gang, "They really think they're something. According to Lou, if we watched a couple of Rambo movies back to back, we might be able to predict their next move."

Lou was going over their little home videos and planned to develop a diagram about the structure of the gang and how many members we were dealing with.

After the attack on the surveillance van, the police were going to put Lou and his wife somewhere else and offered to do the same for me. I declined, telling Nate I'd be at my office for the whole morning.

By ten o'clock, Lou had digitized pictures of the gang members. They were clear and straight on. They were posing with guns. If there were no members who were not on the videos, we were dealing with seven primary players and about thirty runners. The seven were Smithy; Nickel; the fifteen-year-old, now-deceased guard; and four unknowns. The structure was lieutenant, sergeants, and chief arms specialist. The runners were all soldiers. Nickel was lieutenant, Smithy was chief arms specialist, and the guard was one of the soldiers. The rest were unknown. Lou sent this new packet out to the same distribution list as the gang information packet. He would be over to brief our staff at eleven.

Lou looked a little haggard when he arrived. He was wearing a bulletproof vest. He asked me for a cup of my coffee, so I knew he was tired. He did a great job of presenting the update to the staff. Charlene, an adult felony PO, recognized one of the pictures. She had Steve Latrell on open probation. She said she would have a last known address. Char is known for her meticulous chronological records. She also regularly does home visits on her clients. She checked her computer and was back in front of the large group in under a minute. She had printed out a picture from Crim Net for comparison and had printed Latrell's chronological record. He was on probation for felony assault for taking a pool cue to a guy at a bar because the poor guy talked to his girlfriend. The victim ended up with a broken nose and several broken facial bones. The police took Latrell into custody on the original arrest, so he also had a history at the jail where the presentence investigation was completed. He served the first ninety days of his sentence, was released, and never showed up for his first report.

There was a good chance the address he had given was a fake, but it was worth a try. Probation has the authority to search an open client's home without a search warrant, so we had to be involved. Char and Lou requested police backup. The address was in the West Hillside, less than a mile away.

I glanced at my watch. 11:55 A.M. I was supposed to meet Dar at noon. *Shit!* I called her on her cell. She was generous about canceling and told me to call her if things changed.

I took a separate vehicle and met everyone at the last known address of

Steve Latrell. It was a three-story dilapidated Victorian with a turret on the left front corner. I just hate it when houses like this are let go. Latrell's name was still on the mailbox. We had two probation officers, myself, and two squads there for backup. Lou approached the door from the side. Charlene, who is only five feet tall, stood behind him and peered around his shoulder. He gave three strong knocks, and a young woman of about nineteen with stringy blond hair answered the door.

"What can I do you for?"

"Steve Latrell?" Lou asked.

"Sleeping. Can I take a message?"

"We're with probation. We need to get him up. Where is his bedroom?"

"In the back. Can you do this? I mean, doesn't he have rights?" She seemed scared but was trying to show attitude.

"We can," Lou said, and he lowered his voice. "Do you need to put up a fight for show here?"

She nodded, and while gesturing us in with her hand, said, "Get the fuck out of here! He isn't here. You can't go in there."

The police escorted us into the room where Steve was sleeping like a baby. Lou ordered him to get out of bed with his hands in sight. He complied. He had big baggy basketball shorts on. His short brown hair and the soul patch on his chin weren't the only things that made him look like a gangster. He had tattoos covering both arms and his neck. He was handcuffed behind his back and led into the living room. After we searched the couch, we told him to sit down. He put up some resistance to a full house search but knew that it was a condition of his probation and that we would take him into custody and do the search with even more people under a search warrant. He was allowed to watch from the couch under police guard as we began the painstaking job of searching his house.

The TV shows are very inaccurate about how long searches take. It is a huge task if you do it right. Each book needs to be paged through. Every cupboard emptied. Every toilet tank searched. The freezer contents examined. In a probation officer search, the police are only allowed to provide security as we sift through the contents of the house. The first discovery was a Colt 45 under his pillow. Loaded. The second find constituted several bundles of cash wrapped in tinfoil in the freezer. We also found several bags of crack cocaine all divided up into small rocks above a ceiling tile in the bedroom.

Once we found the drugs, the police could take over. It had now become a new crime investigation. I wondered what would have happened if he had not been sleeping. I was also surprised that we didn't find any other weapons. He must have been only a soldier in the gang. We would find out how loyal a soldier he was.

He was booked for third-degree possession with intent to sell and for being a felon in possession of a firearm. He would also be held for violation on his open probation. All this would be used as leverage to get more information on the rest of the gang. He could be held without bail on the violation of probation.

Because Lou was consulting on the case, he would have firsthand access to the interviewing. We were usually not privy to that process. I did feel bad for him, though. He had been working way too much overtime. It hardly showed on him at all. I requested that he keep us posted and wished the officers well. I asked Char to spend some time with Steve's girlfriend to see if she would give any information up about the associates. It was a long shot but worth a try. By the time I left Latrell's house, it was well past three o'clock.

Chapter 9

I CALLED DAR to see if she could make a late lunch. She met me at the Lift Bridge Café. I had to sit waiting for her for ten minutes. I usually hate that, but I was consumed with the details of this gang thing.

I watched two kayakers hurriedly paddling to get under the lift bridge and through the port to avoid meeting any larger vessels. I always joke about how the lift bridge was really designed by an architect's kid playing with tinker toys. It has thousands of metal pieces welded together to form a bridge. The road portion of the bridge lifts up enough to allow all sizes of vessels to pass underneath it into the port. When a thousand-foot, ocean-bound ship passes, it delays traffic to Park Point for a half hour. When a small sailboat passes, traffic is only delayed ten minutes. Sometimes the bridge operator allows several boats to pass in succession, limiting the number of lifts per day.

I resolved to make efficient use of my own time as well. I spent the time waiting for Dar by sorting through some of the facts of the case, trying to make something fall into place. How could we get at the other members of the gang? Could we keep Nichols and Latrell segregated at the jail? If not, could one of them be shipped to a neighboring town's jail? What were they going to try next?

Dar came in, and I offered her a hug. She accepted, stood back, and looked me over.

"You look terrible."

"Thanks! I've missed you, too."

"That is not what I meant, and you know it. Isn't it ironic that you were the one who had to cancel lunch today? I mean, you were always so pissed off at me for messing things up."

"This is starting off on a good foot. I wouldn't exactly say pissed off, more like frustrated. I think it is disrespectful to leave someone waiting. Some things are unavoidable. This was beyond my control."

"I think it is all about how you define 'out of your control.'"

I sat there reflecting on our relationship, about how judgmental I had been about her lateness or just plain forgetting about things. Sometimes I didn't even give her a chance to explain.

"I was judgmental of you."

"So, tell me what's up. Someone broke into the house?"

"I wouldn't say broke in, more like intruded. I think he was trying to deliver a message."

"Did he have a part in the murder of that whole family?"

"There is a pretty good chance of that."

"Jo, he could have been there to kill you."

"That is one possibility."

"At our ... I mean, your house. The dogs, are they OK?"

"They alerted me to the intruder. They may have saved my life."

She paused and examined me.

"So, do you think he was there to kill you?"

"Honestly, I don't know. If he was, he didn't succeed. Can we talk about something else? How have you been? Where are you living?"

She hesitated, as if to consider the wisdom of changing the subject, and begrudgingly answered.

"I'm at the Lester River House. It's a co-op for women. We all share in the housework, cooking, and cleaning. You pay based on your income. It's pretty cool."

"That is so you. I could never do that!"

"I know."

"Dar, I'm sorry about how things ended. I think I had let things build up without talking about them, and well, I never meant to yell at you like that."

"Thanks, I'm sorry, too. I shouldn't have walked out. I just felt so judged all the time. We're very different people—too different. Well, maybe just different in ways that were bad for us as a couple."

"It didn't help that neither one of us was big on talking about things."

"That's true, but I think if we had been talking, we would have been fighting."

"Hard to say."

"Kathy and Donna are well?"

"Quite. Those two are so stable."

I didn't have the nerve to ask her if she was seeing anyone. I'm pretty sure she knew I wasn't. Her instinct to call me at K. & D.'s was right on. We made some uncomfortable small talk, ate warm mushroom salads, and walked out together. The funny thing was, I was still physically attracted to her. How the heck could I be attracted to someone so totally incompatible to me? Weird. It felt good that she didn't seem to hate me.

Back at the office, there was nothing new about the investigation. While Latrell had not asked for a lawyer, he also wasn't talking. I walked down to Char's office. She had just returned from talking to Latrell's girlfriend.

"Her name is Nicole Redding. She has been seeing Steve for six months. She hooked up with him right after he moved here. She knew about the warehouse in Morgan Park, but other than that, she wasn't talking. She denied knowledge of guns or drugs. The apartment was in his name." In an attempt to get information out of her, Char had pointed out to Nicole that she could be charged with being an accessory to Steve's crimes. Even after receiving promises of protection, the woman wouldn't budge.

"Nicole is originally from Virginia, Minnesota. She said she met up with Latrell at a party, but she wouldn't say where. She is three months pregnant." I thanked Char for her report and walked down to my own office.

I took a minute to call my dad. Thankfully, he wasn't home, and I left a message that everything was fine. I had no need for a fishing trip yet.

I also called Kathy about dinner. She let me decide what to get but told me to bring enough for four. They had invited another guest for dinner. Was this what she was hinting about when she asked me if I was ready to date? I couldn't see a way out and wished she hadn't told me about it. I hate blind dates, but this wasn't really a blind date. Just dinner. With two very good friends and someone I had yet to meet.

Chapter 10

I TOOK THE SCENIC route to burn a little time. There were less dead deer on cars in the middle of the week, and I was glad for that. I let my mind go fully into hunter-bashing territory.

My dog Java has a tendency to chase deer. One crossed the driveway in my yard while we were both out one day. He was gaining on it when it suddenly changed direction and came toward him. Java stopped and ran in the other direction. He then jumped up in the air as if he were trying to see over something, sure that the deer was headed in that direction. I was amazed at his attempt to save face. He was a tough guy while it was running away from him, but the minute he was faced with the prospect of a confrontation on equal ground, he ran.

Deer hunting seems even more unfair to me. As I understand it, hunters can feed deer all year, even scent the area and themselves with deer sexual hormones (how gross is that!). Then they sit up in a tree and wait for their prey to come within range and shoot it with a high-powered rifle. In my mind, a fair fight would mean the hunter stalks and runs the deer down, wrestles it to the ground, and kills it with his bare hands.

Java is at great risk during deer season because some hunters think the law says they can legally shoot and kill dogs that chase deer. The law is designed to protect hunters who accidentally shoot dogs they mistake for deer. The thinking that they are justified in shooting a dog for going after their prey pisses me off to no end. Let me at the bugger who takes a shot at my dog.

Thankfully, mental hunter bashing had successfully kept me from thinking about work and the potential setup. I was nearly home, or rather, to my temporary home.

The house was lit up with a cozy fire in the woodstove. The house smelled of chocolate, and I was curious about dessert. The table was set with cloth napkins and a candle ready to light. Holy! This is something, I thought, but did not speak until I had ascertained whether the guest had arrived yet.

"So, who's coming?"

"Her name is Zoey Rundell. She's a new tenure-track Assistant Professor in the Psychology Department at Duluth University. She and Donna have become friends at work. Zoey asked Donna to speak to her Psych 101 class about screening for mental health at the Student Health Clinic. They may do some research together."

"Cool."

I was hopeful this would not be a setup. They were just making new friends. My life was so out of control, I was beginning to lean toward paranoia.

"Are you sure you want me here? I could eat and run."

"Absolutely, I think you'll really like her."

"Do I have time for a walk?"

"Make it quick."

I decided to skip the walk and take a quick shower to clean off the day. I always feel a bit groady after doing a home search, and I hate the smell of latex gloves.

When I got downstairs, Zoey and Donna were sitting in the living room area, and Kathy was in the kitchen getting the Thai food into serving dishes. Donna introduced me as their houseguest. Zoey looked about my height with an athletic build. She was also unmistakably woman. She shook my hand firmly and looked directly into my eyes. Her hand was warm to the touch. She had short, curly brown hair just starting to gray. I put her at around thirty-eight years old. She had stunning green eyes with a glint of mischief in them. It was similar to the spunk I find intriguing in some of the kids I work with.

I found my interest piqued, but my self-talk said: *Don't go there. Your life is too out of control. You don't do well with compatibility screening.* I hate when my self-talk takes on a clinical tone. It means I am trying to detach.

Kathy called us to the table at the end of the introduction. The pad Thai was a big hit. Zoey talked about her work. She had done private practice in New Mexico for about ten years following the completion of her Ph.D. and then transferred to the university setting. She had been in Duluth since the summer session began in June. She ran into Donna in the faculty dining room, and they talked about doing a research study on mental health screening at the Health Center where Donna works. I had heard this before, and her rendition was nearly identical to Donna's. It looked like Donna had found a friend.

I explained my job and was a little uncomfortable talking about it in front of Donna and Kathy. I focused on the good work the juvenile unit does, the groups they run, their undying love of kids, etc., etc., etc.

I caught Kathy rolling her eyes at Donna a bit. She then interrupted me by saying, "And you do have to deal with some pretty unsavory characters in your office, too, right? Like the little shit-heads who murdered that whole family."

This was a little uncharacteristic of her, to display such unguarded anger. We all gave this a moment to settle in. She squirmed.

"Yes, that is true. Up until now, the gangs we have dealt with in Duluth have been relatively small time, and they are usually made up of kids with little or no coping skills who don't fit in. A gang helps kids like that pass for being cool, and it also gives them a place to belong. When they are part of a group, they feel strong. Invincible. As individuals, they are usually pretty insecure, even scared."

I knew I was becoming defensive again but found myself unable to stop. "Way back when I was a juvenile PO, and gangs were beginning to take form in Duluth, I ran a support group for the parents of some of our kids. They were scared about their kids' gang involvement. Essentially the kids were wearing Raiders caps, colors, and jackets, and hanging around in the downtown mall. The parents' assignment for group was to steal an item of their kid's clothing with the gang colors and bring it to group. We then marched down to the mall, put on the clothing, and stood as near to the kids as they would allow. The kids were mortified and kept moving to avoid us. The parents learned about the power they have if they get together, and that the gang kids are still their children, not some abstract concept to be feared." The story ended the discussion, but I could tell Kathy was still feeling edgy.

After dinner, we took a short walk. The moon was waning, so we had to use headlamps. Zoey seemed to really enjoy the experience. She also didn't seem to mind the cold. I wondered what the average temperature in

Albuquerque was in winter. She did overdress, though, which is common for most southerners who venture into Duluth winters.

After the walk, we played a couple of rounds of hearts. My attention was distracted by Zoey, and I did poorly. My friends made good-natured humor about my lack of concentration. The game ended when we were interrupted by a call to my cell phone. I took it in the bathroom.

"Jo Spence."

"Jo, we have a problem." The line went silent for a few seconds. I could picture Nate struggling to put something into words. I let the silence hang there.

"Remember all of those drugs we pulled out of the warehouse in Morgan Park?" Another pause. "They're gone!"

"They're gone? All of them?"

"All of them."

"And they were in your evidence room?"

"Totally by the book."

"How?"

"We don't know. There was no sign of a break-in. The surveillance cameras were just turned away from behind. It's looking like an inside job."

"Holy shit."

"My sentiments exactly."

"Any leads?"

"We're canvassing the building. We have the time pinned down, but so far, nothing. We can't even pin it down to someone who was working."

"Don't you have a sign-out system or something? A guard?"

"Nope, that's just TV stuff. We just have surveillance cameras."

"So, the stuff is back out on the streets?"

"Yup, and the media is gonna eat this shit up. We've called in every available cop to track this down. We also have the jail staked out to see if Nickel's other threats are going to bear any fruit."

"That's right! He said he was going to run the Police Department and the town. The doors to lockup were going to just open up for him. The jail folks don't have access to the PD evidence vault, do they?"

"No, the jail is run by the St. Louis County Sheriff's Department. The evidence vault is DPD. That is a good thought, though. We'll keep a close watch for any contact Nichols has with police or deputies at the jail."

"Can you get someone in undercover at the jail? I mean, have an officer pose as a prisoner?"

"Only if we clear it with the Sheriff, and I doubt he would subject his staff to the scrutiny of the PD. That could set up some pretty bad blood if a cop had to turn in another uniform for something. I also think it would violate the uniform's fifth amendment rights. The perp. would in essence be confessing to a police officer without a Miranda warning. Interesting idea, though."

I could hear the wheels turning in his mind.

"Maybe we could get an informant in the same cell pod with Nichols and see what happens."

"Do you need anything from me?"

"No. I just wanted you to hear it from me."

"Thanks, call if you need anything. I'll put in a fresh battery. Good luck with the media. This is going to look terrible."

I went back out, and Zoey was getting her coat on. I told her how nice it had been to meet her. She replied in kind. Donna walked her out to her car. When Donna returned, we all sat down in front of the fire. Donna looked at me, raised her eyebrows like I was supposed to say something, and said, "Well?"

"What are you asking me?" I knew, but I was playing with her. She just turned her head to the side with a quizzical smile. I could outgame her, or so I thought.

"Was this a date?"

"Did you want it to be?"

"She's a nice woman. She seems bright. Attractive."

"And?"

This was killing me.

"Were you trying to set me up?"

"Do you mind being set up with Zoey?"

"You can be so-o-o-o annoying!"

I looked at Kathy for help, but she just said, "She's good at it."

She definitely had the better of me, and I didn't have the patience for this right now.

"So, call her." Donna had a lot of patience.

"She can call me."

"Great! I'll tell her you want her to call you."

"Aaaargh!"

Chapter 11

WE WENT UP to the TV room. The news coverage was brutal. The DPD had somehow "lost" the proceeds from the biggest drug bust in the tri-state region and was urgently trying to locate the stolen or lost drugs. I confirmed to Kathy and Donna that that is what the call had been about. First thing in the morning, I had to get the probation officers into the schools asking questions. Someone out there had to know something. I would also have to talk to the adult unit supervisor to see if his agents could turn over any rocks.

As I settled into bed with my two boys, I thought about this whole Zoey thing. What would this do to my friendship with Donna? What if things didn't work out? What if they did? Shit! She was attractive and seemed to have her life together. God, I hate dating.

I always dream just as I'm falling asleep. This one was interesting. Zoey and I were walking on my trail. She stopped on the trail, turned around, and kissed me. I kissed her back. I woke up. Shit! Shit! Shit!

As soon as I fell asleep again, I had another dream. I was walking to work along the Lakewalk trail. I was carrying a briefcase I did not recognize. It was leather and quite full. I had the urge to look inside to see what I was carrying, but I didn't. I kept on walking. The air was fresh and clean. Lake Superior was a steel blue. The sky was a deeper blue with billowy white clouds. Only a few people were out. It was cold enough that I could see smoke coming from chimneys. The city up on the hill was still.

Suddenly, I began to see graffiti everywhere: on the mural next to the scenic tourist railroad tracks, on the lift bridge itself, and even on the walkway. Then a young man in baggy pants and a watch cap jumped out onto the trail, carrying a knife. I just smiled at him and began reaching into the briefcase. I felt calm and able to handle the situation. I still didn't know what was in the briefcase. As I opened it up to reach inside, I woke up.

I was annoyed. My urge was to fall right back to sleep to get the rest of the story, but that had never worked. I told myself that it was a dream. Not real. I lay there thinking about the dream and what it meant. Could it be that I already had the solution to the new gang problem in Duluth? I didn't have a clue what the contents of that briefcase might be. Someone else held all the answers, but it wasn't me.

I got up and went downstairs to rummage around in my friends' fridge. Helping myself to their food felt both strange and nurturing. I knew they wouldn't care. I found some ice cream in the freezer and filled a little bowl. I softened it up a bit in the microwave and sat myself down in front of the fire. My pups were begging shamelessly. I have a habit of letting them lick the bowl. Consequently, they stare at my every bite.

OK, Nichols said he would run this town, including the Police Department. He expected the doors to lockup to open wide for him. His bangers didn't know that he had been transferred to the jail, so they had attempted to break him out of detention. The drugs from the warehouse raid were missing, and it looked like an inside police job. The bandits were heavily armed and had financial resources. They also used the drugs they sold, made home movies of themselves, and watched porn. Their gang symbols were adaptations from the Disciples gang, but none of their graffiti had shown up around town. They were highly organized, and we weren't sure how big the gang was. Their colors were black and blue, like the Disciples. They were mostly white kids, but there were adults, too. Some of them were brothers. Nichols was in jail, as was Steve Latrell. Latrell had been to adult jail here within the past sixty days. Both came from Detroit. Nichols seemed to be narcissistic. What else was I missing? Where was the older Nichols brother, "Smithy"? He had to be the arms specialist.

I got up and refilled my ice cream bowl, this time setting it down and letting the fire soften it. The other suspects in the video had not been identified, but the pictures were in every squad. The police were watching the jail. Chances were the gang would try to break Nichols out of there, or a guard might be working from the inside. There was definitely a leak somewhere. The jail staff had been alerted. Someone tossed my office looking for Lou's address, then tossed his house looking for something. Then the intruder came to my house, presumably to kill me or to deliver a message. What was his mission? Why had they sent someone to Lou's? Lou had Nichols on an open file. Lou has gang knowledge. Gangs both fear and respect him. Lou is NOT the inside guy. No way.

By the time I had finished my train of thought, my ice cream was nearly a puddle, just the way I like it. I finished it off and trudged up to bed. I slept right through the alarm. Kathy or Donna must have come in and turned it off. At eight o'clock, I padded downstairs. Coffee was in a thermos, with a note from Kathy saying she had an appointment and to enjoy. I skipped my ritual walk, hit the shower, and sped off to work.

Chapter 12

I MADE IT to work by 9:30. The funeral for the Toivunen family was scheduled for 11 A.M. at the Hillside Community Center. Lou was in the office updating the staff about the missing drugs. I grabbed him and asked for specifics. He didn't have much. I asked him about the plans to cover the funeral. He said that there would be a strong police presence in the Center in plain clothes, as well as squads outside.

I also inquired about his sleep. He looked better, but still a little ragged. He had slept fine. The PD had put him up in a suite on the top floor of the Radisson Hotel. "Nice digs," according to Lou.

"Lou, did you ever figure out why they broke into your house?"

"I don't know. A message, I guess. The thinking of these guys is all screwed up. It's not making any sense."

"Did you find anything missing?"

"Not a thing."

"Any instincts on who is the inside guy?"

"Not a one. There are some guys on the force I get a creepy feeling about, but I can't imagine any of them being tied to a gang that is capable of murdering a whole family."

"That's the hard part. I want to see the takedown if and when they find him."

"Me, too."

"See you at the funeral?"

"Right next to you."

"Thanks, Lou."

The Central Hillside Community Center is in a huge old rehabbed school. The memorial services were held in the auditorium. The audience of nearly three hundred contained Hillside residents, police, school folks, and friends of the family. There were no immediate family members left to attend. Community activists took the opportunity to turn the occasion into a "let's reclaim our city" rally. The police handed out pictures of the bandits and asked people to call 911 if they saw anyone or anything, and to avoid contact. Police were visibly scanning the crowd for weapons. It took me a minute to realize that their fear was that everyday citizens were carrying guns, ready to "protect" themselves and their loved ones. That also scared me.

When the service ended, I gathered Don, Char, Lou, and Nate, and asked them to join me at It's a Perk, my second favorite coffee shop in town, to discuss things. They were happy to comply. I sensed their feelings of helplessness about the whole situation.

Everyone was quiet for a while as we huddled around the coffee. Then I took the lead.

"So, where do you think they took the drugs? I mean, there were a lot of drugs there. Where would they hide them?"

Nate spoke up. "My guess is that the drugs are still in the vehicle they transported them in. The vans at the warehouse all had Detroit plates. That's a place to start. We also have those pictures everywhere. I mean everywhere. We'll get a tip soon."

Just like in the movies, Nate's cell phone rang as if on cue. When he hung up, he said a tip had come in. "You'll never believe where it came from-an eight-year-old girl. The girl's mom brought her down to the station because of what she had been talking about. I gotta fly. Lou, are you coming? Jo?"

"I'm in."

"Me, too."

At the station, we were introduced to Jane Sanders and her daughter Christine. Christine was quite the kid: very bright and definitely a talker. She said hello to each of us as we were introduced. She was small for her age with bright orange hair, and an attitude. She seemed the kind of kid who isn't scared of anyone, but who is smart enough to avoid trouble.

Christine and her mom lived next door to some of the guys whose pictures had been on the news. She went on to say that the neighbors had people going in and out all the time, and Christine had been keeping an eye on them from her window at night. She said they smoked a lot of pot, explaining that she knew what it was from the DARE (Drug Abuse Resistance Education) program at school. She could write well enough to give us a statement, but we didn't think we would need one to get a warrant. The mom confirmed that there had been a lot of traffic, but she didn't recognize the pictures.

After the interview, Lou and I bought Christine and her mom soft drinks in the cop shop coffee shop. Nate was chasing down a warrant. This kid was a stitch. She wanted to know all about the case. Were these the guys who had stolen all of the drugs back from the police? Would she get a reward? How about an award then? Maybe she would be a police officer some day. Her mom just sat there quietly. I wondered whether she was depressed or just tired.

The police were setting up a plan for the raid. Access to the information was limited due to the previous drug heist. The SWAT team was called in. I was afraid for the lives of these bad guys. Every cop was keyed up to the max. The boys in blue were not thrilled about looking like idiots for losing the drugs. However this played out, it was not going to be pretty.

Chapter 13

I DECIDED to go along as an observer. The address was in the East Hillside area. As usual, my mind wandered during the drive. The East Hillside was the third area to be developed in Duluth. The first, interestingly enough, was the West Hillside. Houses were built into a steep hill. Materials had been carried to the work sites by a rail system, and by goats. It baffled me why Duluth's earliest residents would build on the steepest part of a city in that day and age. Maybe it had to do with the excellent views of Lake Superior. The East Hillside, developed after the Central Hillside area, is not as steep as the other two, but it also does not command quite the view of the Port or the famous lift bridge. Houses for sale in the eastern part of Duluth are sometimes advertised as having a lake view, when only a slice of the lake is visible from an attic window. Several creeks meander through the East Hillside area in their search for Lake Superior. There are also a couple of parks with recreational trails, so it is still a nice neighborhood to raise a family in. Most of the houses in this area were built between 1900 and 1920.

The suspect's house was at 1544 East Fifth Street. It was a large, three-story house built long and narrow, only four feet from the neighboring house where our eight-year-old tipster lived. I could see why it was easy for her to spy on the activities next door. Lou and I drove by the house and parked a block past it. We then walked within view. The SWAT team was dressed in camouflage and wearing helmets with big plastic-looking shields. A team of five rammed the front door as another team of five rammed the rear entrance. Several uniformed officers maintained a perimeter around the house so that citizens would not be endangered. I heard shots, yelling, more shots. Then more yelling, and finally silence. I held my breath. Lou elbowed me and told me to breathe. I took in a big breath and slowly exhaled. I could see helmets running throughout the house in and out of every room. I presumed that they were securing the building. Several officers walked three men out of the building. The men/boys were belly chained and shackled. The first officer yelled, "All clear. Three in custody. Two inside." I presumed the two inside were dead.

We waited several minutes and then approached Police Chief Knight. He briefed us: "Three individuals were in the living room playing a video game. Two men pulled weapons and failed to respond to commands to drop them. One of them turned off his safety, and officers fired on the two armed suspects. The third individual dropped to the floor and covered. The other two were in an upstairs bedroom, unarmed, and they surrendered without a fight. A preliminary search has turned up keys to a U-Haul moving van, several handguns, and one sawed-off shotgun. We found evidence of recreational use of crack, powder cocaine, and pot, all three drugs in small amounts. All five match the video pictures. They also have sweet little matching tats covering both arms. Gang symbols. We have enough for arrests for possession and resisting. We can pull some facts from their activities in the video and crank out a few more charges. One of the perps we have in custody is a juvenile. The rest are adults, including the two who were shot. None of them matches the description of the Nichols brother. We'll get something out of them and locate that van. We can call U-Haul to find out who rented the van and make some progress there."

By the time we got back to the office, it was after six o'clock. There was no one except the intensive unit to brief. I filled them in on our progress. Lou was going to the PD to see if he could help out with the investigation, document the tattoos, and try to get a clearer picture of the hierarchy and how these guys fit into it. We needed to get a handle on who was still out there.

When I got to their house, Kathy and Donna had lasagna in the oven and had waited for me. They both had conspiratorial smirks on their faces when I talked about how my alarm hadn't awakened me that morning. Kathy asked how the funeral had gone. I explained how worked up the community was and that I was afraid of vigilante justice. I was worried that some not-so-balanced citizens could mistake regular children for gangsters and hurt innocent kids. Lots of kids looked and dressed like gangsters these days. The baggy jeans, caps, and starter jackets were in fashion. To the average citizen, they all looked alike.

Donna said that there was a message from Zoey asking me to call her. Donna got another smirk on her face and just looked at me innocently.

I built up my nerve and asked Donna, "Why do you think we would be compatible?"

"I don't really know, Jo. I just sense it. It seems good to me."

"How well do you know her?"

"I talk to her every day."

I bolstered myself again. I was determined to break the habit of not asking the hard questions.

"Have you thought through how this might impact our relationship? Our friendship? I mean, what if things don't work out? That could get complicated. What if things do work out? That could get complicated, too."

"I'm not worried about it. You are not a jerk. She is not a jerk. Either it will work out, or it won't. Whatever happens, I'll deal with it. You and I will just have to figure it out either way."

She made it sound so easy. Could it really be that easy?

After dinner, Kathy and I walked the dogs. She seemed to think that Donna could really be that clear about boundaries and that I could trust her not to distance herself from me if things didn't work out. She also said that I should call Zoey. I contemplated the timing of it. I was consumed with this investigation. I couldn't even live at my own house because of it. I thanked her again for letting me stay with them and told her that the case was progressing.

Even though we didn't have the older Nichols boy in custody yet, I longed to go to my house to see if everything was all right. Leaving my house may have kept me safe, but it did nothing to keep my house safe. Kathy sensed my unease and put an arm around me. I asked her to accompany me to my house after the walk to check it out. She agreed.

From the outside, things looked fine. I gathered my mail, and we trudged up the walk. The motion light activated correctly, and that reassured me. The house was warm inside, and the broken window was fixed. There was no sign of the break-in. Buddy had left me a bill indicating that he had had to replace the entire window. It was right at the amount of my homeowner's insurance deductible. I was just glad it was fixed; the damage could have been worse. I grabbed some clean clothes and just stood there looking around at my house. I had the urge to clean it to reclaim it. Kathy allowed me some time to deal with my feelings. Later, I thought.

In the car on the way back, she asked me what I had been thinking about. I told her I wanted to clean. She laughed and said, "You are a little compulsive, aren't you?"

I laughed and said, "I should get points for resisting."

I called Zoey from an upstairs bedroom. She invited me to dinner at her house at 7 P.M. Friday night. I told Kathy and Donna I would be late because I had a dinner date. I was more afraid of this dinner date than of anything about the case. I didn't tell them that, though. We played a game of hearts, and I went to bed exhausted.

I started to dream as soon as I fell asleep. I was walking my boys in an open field. The field was planted in some kind of ornamental grass: acres and acres of green grass. I ran full throttle with the dogs, and then rolled and tumbled and wrestled with each of them. We all lay down together for a sweet nap in the sun. The clouds were sparse. It was summer, and the sky was an intense blue. The sun was warm on my face. Cocoa was sleeping with his head on my shoulder. Java was at my feet.

Then, out of nowhere, it began to rain. The raindrops were blue. When they hit us, they melted into vapor. When they hit the grass, they turned it brown. I got up to run away from the grass, but my dogs just stood there. Java tried to run, but every time he put his paw down on the brown grass, it hurt him. He just looked at me. His eyes were pleading with me to stay with him. His face turned into Lou's.

I woke up. Stunned. What the hell was that about? What did Lou have to do with the missing drugs? Could he be involved somehow? Maybe my subconscious mind was warning me not to overlook the possibility. Shit!

I went downstairs to see if there was any ice cream left. I vowed to replenish their supply. Sure enough, there was a fresh container of Haagen Dazs vanilla Swiss almond. I resumed my thinking position in front of the fire with my two begging dogs and began to ponder.

Again I thought about all of the facets of this case and also whether Lou could have played into any of it. There was a leak and a thief on the inside of the PD. Lou had full access to the PD, but Lou was not living beyond his means. He had a viable source of extra income. Nichols had said that he would run the PD. Or was it "Own the PD"? I'd have to check that out. Lou was not part of the PD. The likely mole was there. I didn't know enough about the inside workings of the PD to know who was most likely crooked. Lou was working on it, I felt sure. Police Chief Knight was most likely too removed to know. I'm sure Nate had some theories.

* * * *

On Friday morning when I got to work, there was a message on my work machine to call Nate. The police had located the U-Haul van. It had been under armed guard. They wounded the guard and recovered the drugs. I asked him if he had a theory about the leak. He did but couldn't talk to me about it over the phone. The police were planning a trap to flush out the traitor. They had installed guards of their own to protect the drugs. FBI agents, affectionately called "Feebies," would help out with that. They would also be heading up the trap. From the diagram Lou had put together, Smithy Nichols and one other high-ranking gang member were left to be located. The jail had cooperated in keeping the gang associates separated there. The jail was also under tight surveillance. This was doing a number on the PD overtime budget. The mayor wouldn't argue, though. This whole thing had been a PR nightmare.

I spent an hour calling around about security systems. I found one that could dial into 911 after a call went out to my home and cell simultaneously. It also had an arm/disarm feature. It was going to eat a chunk of my savings, but I authorized the installation.

I wasn't sure what I was going to do about the boys yet, but this was a start. The security company would have the system installed in three days. By Monday morning, I would be in my own house. I was kind of enjoying the company and care of Kathy and Donna, but I also didn't want to wear out my welcome. I was feeling relatively secure, assuming that most of the gang was in custody. I could not ignore, however, the possibility that the intrusion was a botched hit ordered by Nichols and that someone would come back to finish the job.

I was struggling with why I would be perceived as such a threat. Nichols was a nut with a god complex, and he seemed manic. Methamphetamine freaks can get that way, but they eventually calm down after they clean up. Some bipolar clients self-medicate with all kinds of drugs. The remote possibility also existed that he was getting something in lockup. We couldn't urinalysis test while clients were on pretrial status. I'd have to make sure we got a psychological on him for his predisposition investigation.

I found myself thinking about the dream I had had about Zoey. I wondered how things would go on our first date. I spent the rest of the day catching up on what the staff had been doing all week. Court was business as usual. Predispositional investigations were being completed. Violations of probation were being processed. School, office, and home checks were taking place. The groups were quite alive with the talk about what was going on. The PO's were capitalizing on this to get the kids to think about their lives, their choices, and the subsequent consequences.

Midafternoon, I took a walk to the Courthouse to talk to Judge Manning. Over the years, I have learned that an occasional visit to him pays big dividends to my unit, and to the kids we are trying to help. In the five minutes it took to walk the two blocks, I thought back on my history with Judge Manning. A distinguished looking, middle-aged man, he could easily pass for thirty-five. He has carefully groomed dark hair and a goatee. As the primary Juvenile Court Judge for the past twenty-five years, he has been passionate about kids and has assumed a personal level of responsibility for crime in the community and the welfare of the CHIPS (child in need of protective services) clients, but he is often tough on the professionals who come before him, calling attention to problems.

He and I have gone nose to nose many times about how he treats PO's in the courtroom. He is particularly tough on new PO's. He has a tendency to take his frustrations out on the professionals when a case is hard or when he can't do what he wants to do for technical reasons. The new PO's eventually toughen up and can even help him laugh about his reactions. He respects the ones who come right back at him, and consequently, we have carved out a relationship of trust and respect over the years. He also has a good handle on the various levels of kids who come before him. He is good about not labeling or overreacting to low-risk kids, but he comes down hard on the kids who need it.

I found myself comparing him to some of the other judges and prosecutors who are either too liberal or too conservative. Liberal judges lose sight of victim impact and community safety, and are overfocused on helping the offenders change, while conservative judges overfocus on punishment and alienate themselves from the offenders, jeopardizing rehabilitation. Judge Manning has a good balance. He is also research based in his approach. I considered him to be an ally—one with whom I wanted to keep the lines of communication open.

I entered the Courthouse from the front of the building. I have never tired of the historic marble pillars, the high ceilings, and the ornately carved oak handrails. I took in the sound of clients and lawyers preparing for their hearings in the marble hallways, and the sharp click of my footsteps as I walked down the hall. Judge Manning's clerk motioned me in as she glanced up from her computer. He was reading what looked to be a brief and had stopped to watch a thousand-foot salty slip under the lift bridge from his viewpoint on the fourth floor. We sat there in silence until the ship had passed into the bay.

He set the brief down and asked how the investigation was going. He knew that I knew how much I could tell him without making him have to remove himself from any future related cases. I told him we had most of the major players rounded up and were looking for the last two.

He asked me how I was holding up. I told him I was in good hands but missed my house. He gave me a couple of good reports on the activities of my juvenile probation officers, and we parted ways.

Probation was next on my list, and I took the stairs down a flight and headed straight for Chief Long's office. He was buried in what I presumed to be our budget. His desk was strewn with paper. Two stress lines were etched deeply above his nose, and he was looking all of his sixty years. His gray hair was thinning, and he seemed to have lost a little weight since I had last seen him. He was wearing his characteristic suspenders under a medium gray suit with a white pressed shirt. Having worked for the agency for thirty-five years, he knew all of the 230 staff that made up our organization.

"Hey, Chief. What's new?"

"You tell me. I could use a break from all of this." He gestured toward the paper covering his desk.

"Glad to be of help."

I filled him in on the recapture of the drugs and the number of apprehended gang members. He asked how I was holding up and whether I had received any new threats. I told him no, but that I had a security system going in. He mentioned that he would approach the board about at least partial reimbursement for it, and for the window expense as well. That was a nice surprise. I think it was the only joyful thing he was going to do all day. I felt bad for him. I vowed to myself to have him and his wife out for a nice dinner. He didn't have a homophobic bone in his body. His oldest son was gay, but for some reason didn't include Chief Long in his life much. I think the Chief liked to spend time with me in part because of that.

My final stop was the City Building located just east of the Courthouse, one of the three buildings that make up the Civic Center complex. I lingered on the bench that encircles the Statue of Sieur du Luth and took in the gardens and the enormity of the Courthouse. For some reason, I noticed the delicate Roman style letters stating "Public Service in Pursuit of Knowledge and Justice." What does it say about me that I have never stopped to think deeply about the phrase? Prior to that moment, I could not have even told you what the phrase was. I wondered if anyone who worked in the building could. Perhaps the guy who had to clean it. I realized my meandering thoughts had turned to cleaning, and I shook them off, wondering why I was procrastinating going into Police headquarters.

My goals were to catch up on the interrogation of the three new custodial suspects and to check on Lou. I found Nate in his office. He said Lou was meeting with the guys individually at the jail and at the detention center. He was trying to build rapport to see what they had to say. Lou approached them as a PO trying to decide if they would qualify for some type of supervised release. In reality, there was no way in hell these guys were getting out.

Nate was working on the leak problem. I couldn't get him to budge an inch about the trap, but he thought out loud with me about possibilities. I think he was glad to have an ear from outside his agency that he could bounce things off of without it getting back somehow.

Jim Stocke was a beat cop who had been demoted from sergeant last year and moved from narcotics. He was caught with drugs in his possession on two occasions. Policy is that any drugs need to be logged procedurally as evidence and accounted for in reports. His story was that he was planning on doing it but had not gotten to it yet. Officers are not drug tested as a routine employment procedure, and subsequent testing proved negative. The drugs he was caught with could easily be metabolized in twenty-four hours.

The department had received several complaints against Officer John

Moore about possible missing money after he had responded to dead body calls. The money had allegedly been taken by Moore out of the purses or wallets of the corpses. If the allegations were true, this guy was very cold. The accusations couldn't be proven, though, because he was first on the scene and had to clear folks out of the area while he secured the residence to determine cause of death.

"This is just too hard to figure out based on speculation. It's a big department." Nate said.

"Any chance that it is someone outside the department? Connected somehow?"

"That's a long shot. The individual or individuals who took those drugs knew where every camera was and avoided ones that led to the area. My guess is that it was one of us."

"I guess it is up to the Feds to turn over that stone," I concluded.

"Well, there is another way to investigate this. We're running all the names and addresses of our known suspects in the Computer Aided Database System. Every call to every residence, responses to complaints, or street interactions are logged into this system on scene. The officers can also retrieve information from it in the squads. We can determine which officers have responded to calls involving these guys, and see who or what pops up. I have Lieutenant Hayes on this. She is at my level in another department, and I trust her. We have a chance of narrowing the field."

"Can I ask when the sting is going to go down?"

"Sorry, Jo."

I finished out the day by calling my dad. "Hey, Dad, what's up?"

"One good thing about this situation is that you call me more. Why do you have to have a reason?"

I didn't have a good answer for him, so I just let the silence hang there.

"Lois and I are going to go on a gambling cruise tomorrow with some friends. We'll be gone for a week. Is everything OK with you? I see the police and that PO got the drugs back." He put the emphasis on the PO.

"Yes, they did. Things are moving along here. I should be back in my house by next week."

"Great! Glad to hear it, sweetheart. We love you."

"I love you, too, Dad."

It did unnerve me a little that he was being so sweet. Maybe it was all a part of aging. While I didn't have to worry about him reading the on-line newspaper and panicking for a while, I did wonder to myself why I didn't call him more.

Chapter 14

THE TIME FOR my date was fast approaching. I had successfully avoided thinking about it for most of the day. I brought my car to the drive-through car wash and made my way up the hill to Zoey's place.

Zoey lived in an area near the University. I wondered whether she walked to work. There were nice Tudor and traditional homes in this neighborhood interspersed with college rental properties. I thought about how the college houses can contain as many as eight students under one roof. The city tries to regulate the number of bodies with rental permits, but the students find many creative ways around the regulations. Landlords want to get paid while avoiding damaged houses from too many keg parties. A new city ordinance allows a landlord to be fined if the police are called to a college rental house more than three times in a semester. I don't think it has cut down on the parties much. The drinking age in Duluth is twenty-one. Most of the college freshmen are eighteen, and graduate at twenty-two or twenty-three. The problem is obvious. Campus police issue hundreds of consumption tickets, and they run them through the courts. Some students see them as badges of honor. Judges tend to throw frequent offenders in jail for ten days over the semester break.

It occurred to me that I have a jaded view of this city because of my job, so I tried to clear my mind as I walked up to Zoey's house. She lived in a cute little Tudor with an arch over the front door and a dormer upstairs. The walkway was brick.

It had begun to snow lightly. The scene was made more inviting by Christmas lights strung over the entryway.

I hesitated before ringing the bell. Was I ready for this? How would I know if it was not right? I have not had good judgment in the past. Would I ever develop an internal gauge for compatibility?

I rang the bell. She came to the door with a smile and let me in. She took my coat and ushered me into the kitchen. The house had open archways between the living room, dining room, and kitchen. The floors were light maple, and the walls were an eggshell white. She had watercolor paintings in the living room and a large weaving in the dining room. The kitchen floor was a Mexican-style, solid-color tile, with a colorful back-splash behind white-tiled countertops. I smelled something spicy in the oven.

"Mmm … smells good."

"Oven-baked burritos. My great grandmother's recipe. She was Chicana. I suspect the ingredients have been Americanized quite a bit, though."

"Where did your green eyes come from?"

"You are observant, aren't you? My dad had green eyes. His grandmother was Austrian. That whole side of the family has similar eyes."

"They are unique, and beautiful."

(Shit, why did I say that? Slow down here, Jo. You don't even know this woman. Think before you speak!)

She just smiled and thanked me, offered me a glass of red wine, and continued to prepare an appetizer made with tortillas that had a red sauce, cheese, and light spices. We took the appetizer and moved into the living room. I noticed that there was no television. We sat on the floor in front of a gas fireplace with our backs to the couch. She filled me in on the details about how she ended up in Duluth, saying that she found the summers in New Mexico too harsh and the lack of seasons barren. She had taken a college vacation in the Boundary Waters and fallen in love with the country. She had a curiosity about the snowy winters here, but she was not without fear. The first snow she had seen had been three nights before. She thought it was beautiful, but she was terrified to drive in it. She had purchased a shovel, mega winter clothing, and was excited about the falling snow outside. It had really begun to come down. With the wind rising, it was fast approaching white-out conditions. I was a little worried about how I was going to get home in all of this, but I was happy to be able to see her experience real snow for the first time. That would be a treat no matter how the night turned out.

The oven-baked burritos were excellent. Peppers, beans, cheese, and rice all baked up in one pan. It was such a simple meal. I would have to try to recreate this dish. Over dinner, Zoey asked about my work and the current case. I found it very easy to talk to her; it was nice not to have to downplay things as I did with my dad and with Kathy and Donna. I told her about the case, leaving out names, and just talked and talked. I even revealed to her my fears about Lou and my conflict about those fears. It occurred to me in the middle of the meal that I wasn't nervous anymore.

When we finished dinner, I helped with the dishes. She put Norah Jones on the CD player, and we did the dishes in relative silence. I noted that she was sensitive to how we worked together while seemingly giving herself over to the music. I did the same. It was almost like a dance—a lot like how Kathy and I work together on projects. We don't have to talk about how to work together; we just do it. I love companionable silences.

The snow was really coming down outside, and I couldn't see my car. I suggested that we go outside to play a bit. I didn't have snow pants, but I did have a long coat, hat. and gloves. We went out and just stood on the front walk watching the snow.

"Does it always snow this hard? Is this normal?"

"No, this is coming down unusually hard. It looks like we are in for a blizzard. Sometimes in a blizzard you can't tell how much snow there really is because it blows around so much. This is a lot of snow, though. It's already three inches deep. Let's take my car out and give you some driving lessons."

"Really? OK."

We took the Range Rover to the faculty parking lot at the University. On the way over, I was wondering how much snow we were going to get and how the heck I was going to get home. I really wanted to play in it a bit longer, though. The parking lot was deserted, so I demonstrated stopping, starting, and whipping donuts. She took the wheel with a little trepidation, but that same mischievous grin soon appeared. She practiced stopping, starting, pumping the brakes, and turning in the snow. When it came time for the donuts, we took it out of four-wheel drive, and she did one tentative donut followed by another. Then she did a three-donut spree while yelling "Yee-haw." It was a blast. Then I showed her how to steer a skidding car while pumping the brakes. When the lesson was over, we struggled to make it back to her house.

By then, it had snowed eight inches. That is a lot of snow, especially for "in town." With Lake Superior, there can be a six-inch difference in the amount of snowfall between town and the North Shore. In the back of my mind, I was wondering how a slumber party would go over.

Back at the house, I told her that we had one more lesson to complete before going inside: We had to make snow angels. This time I didn't demonstrate but just talked her through it. She lay down and moved her arms and legs as instructed. When she got up, she squealed with delight. It was actually hard to see the angel due to the blowing, but we made several before heading inside.

Once inside, I asked her if I could use her phone. I called Kathy and Donna. Kathy asked how things were going. I guessed that Donna's ear was also glued to the phone. I told her we were having a great time. I described the driving lessons and the snow angels. I also told them I was not calling to give them a play-by-play.

"How much snow do you have there?" I asked.

"Tons. Almost a foot. Have you listened to the weather report? This is going to be one heck of a storm. We may get over three feet by the time it's over. You better not try to drive home. The weather service has issued a severe winter storm warning. All motorists are asked to stay put."

I wasn't sure I trusted them. They had set this little date up.

"There is no way you should try to drive in this stuff. You have to stay. Don't worry about a thing. The boys are all safe and tucked in. We are having our own little date here, too."

I could picture the impish grins on their faces. I'm sure they high-five'd after hanging up. Zoey had gone upstairs and returned with a pair of clean sweats for me, since my pants were soaked. I thanked her and asked her if she had a radio or a TV. She walked over and turned the radio on. D. and K. were not exaggerating. This storm was going to break records. I didn't know how to bring this up to Zoey.

"Zoey, how do you feel about having a houseguest? I don't want to risk driving home in this."

"Wow, this will be some first date. No problem. It will be fun."

She went into the kitchen and came back with cappuccino. What a treat. We enjoyed it in relative silence for a while, our gazes alternately enjoying the fire and then the snow.

"So, when should I shovel?"

She really didn't know anything about winter.

"Well, in a storm you can shovel several times or do it all at once when it lets up. In a blizzard, you have to wait until the snow lets up. If you shovel during a blizzard, the wind will just undo all of your work. This is one of those times."

We sat in front of the fire for a long time, talking about the various research projects she had been working on. She had done research, which she found fascinating, even before she began teaching. "It's like thinking new thoughts." That is how she and Donna got to be friends. They struck up a conversation one day, and that sparked a common interest in doing a study utilizing the students Donna sees at the Student Health Center.

At the next pause in conversation, I bravely asked her to fill me in on how and when she came out. She nodded and began. "I was seventeen. I was shortstop on the softball team in high school, and my best friend played second base. We were inseparable. We both had boyfriends and double-dated a lot. I found myself getting jealous about the time she spent with him. I struggled a lot with it. It took a long time for me to get clear about my feelings for her. I also didn't know what to do with those feelings. I didn't want to be gay. One day, we were all at a party in the desert, sitting around a campfire drinking cheap wine. The boys were being raucous, and she and I were huddled together under one blanket. We just held hands under the blanket. It was so sweet. She felt the same way I did. We both broke up with our boyfriends and slowly explored a physical relationship. We were secretive about it with the rest of our friends and our parents. That was very hard. I was head over heels in love, and I wanted to spend all of my time with her. I desperately wanted to be out in the open, but she couldn't handle it. She went back to her old boyfriend and away to college the following year. I was crushed. First love is so hard. I heard that she is with a woman now, twenty-two years later."

That put Zoey at forty. I had wondered which of us was older.

"So, you are forty. When is your birthday?"

"July. Why?"

"Ha, you are older!"

"By how much?"

"Three months."

She just laughed at me and said, "Obviously more mature, too."

Chapter 15

PRESUMABLY THE SNOW was putting a damper on all of the gang activities. I thought of the poor jail and detention staff who were going to have to pull all-night shifts, possibly longer. When I worked at the juvenile detention center, I once had to work two and one-half days straight during a storm. That was not fun. I had to pull a mattress into one of the offices to get some sleep.

Thinking about work reminded me to check my silent cell, and I realized that the battery was nearly dead. I asked Zoey if I could forward my calls to her home phone. She agreed.

She then asked if I wanted to watch a movie.

"Sure. What do you have?"

"Well, I stopped at the video store on my way home and picked up a couple. Have you seen *Better than Chocolate* or *Like Water for Chocolate?*" I had seen them both and thought they were excellent choices.

"Where is your TV?"

"It's in my bedroom, but I promise not to attack you."

"Is that going to be a problem for you?"

Again, she just smiled at me and said, "There is that maturity thing again."

I was a little nervous about the video in bed idea, since both movies were quite sensual, but I went along with the idea.

Thankfully, her bed was king-sized. We propped about twenty pillows up behind each of us and turned on *Better than Chocolate*. We laughed, commented on the baby dykes, and cried. It was a great movie. I had momentarily forgotten that I was lying in her bed watching a lesbian flick. At the end, though, I became quite aware of it, and I found myself aching for her. She sensed my discomfort and got up to use the bathroom. When she returned, I was standing. I asked her what she had in mind about the sleeping arrangements. She had a guest room and a new spare toothbrush. She showed me to my room. While I lay in the next room aching a little, I wondered what she was feeling.

My thoughts raced. *OK, so you are attracted to her. That doesn't mean anything. Well, it is something, but you get so blinded by sex. See what else there is. There is time. Just get to know her.*

I had a difficult time falling asleep. When I awoke, it was fully light out. I stepped to the window in awe of the snow. It was still coming down. This was some storm. Visibility was so bad that I couldn't see the ground from the upstairs, and the trees I could see were bent over with a steady wind.

I padded downstairs. Zoey was up and offered me coffee, which I gratefully accepted.

"Did Donna tell you about my love of coffee?"

"You mean your coffee addiction?"

"OK, my coffee addiction."

"Yes, she mentioned it."

I offered to make breakfast. She accepted with a hand gesture. Rummaging through her fridge, I decided to make a garbage omelet. I call it a garbage omelet because I use whatever is in the fridge. She actually had some great ingredients. I took my time. Why not? We weren't going anywhere. As she watched me from the kitchen table, I sautéed some mushrooms and onions in garlic butter. Then I poured them into the eggs and melted in mozzarella, Parmesan, and Colby jack cheese, covering the whole shebang with a drizzle of the butter/mushroom mix.

She actually let out a little moan as she ate.

"Stop that," I said.

I was a little embarrassed by having it affect me. She just smirked. This was going to be a hard day. She did dishes while I showered.

The snow was not letting up. I estimated a foot and a half had fallen since the previous day. When I went downstairs, the radio was on, and the report confirmed a foot and a half of snow in town, two feet up the North Shore, and three feet on the South Shore in Wisconsin. It was record-breaking snow, with more expected. The storm was not supposed to subside until Monday. I was more than a little nervous about spending such a long first date with Zoey.

I was also nervous about how attracted to her I was becoming. I wondered what was going on with her. She again sensed my fear and said, "Want to go out and play?"

I laughed and replied, "You are fearless."

"Yes, yes I am."

Chapter 16

WE DONNED OUR OUTDOOR wear and ventured out. Neither of us had a clue about what we were going to do. I grabbed a shovel and made my way out to my Rover on the street. A drift had covered the entire rear of my vehicle. All that was visible was the front half of the roof.

The task looked hopeless. Even if we managed to dig it out, it would be buried again within an hour. We tried a couple more snow angels and then decided to try to build a snow fort. The snow wasn't sticky, so we used shovels and built a huge mound. We then began to dig through the middle of the mound to make a tunnel. She began on one end, and I on the other. After we successfully met in the middle, we just sat there in our woman-made tunnel and watched our breath. Again, I felt an immense attraction to her. My mind raced to kissing her. Feeling the warmth of her mouth in the cold. I literally shook it off, and said, "OK, time to go in."

We went inside, stripped out of the winter wear, and sat in front of the gas fireplace again. She asked me what I had been thinking out there. I looked at her, thought for a minute, and decided to tell her. I remembered my vow not to repeat the Dar scenario of not talking about things and not asking the hard questions. She was asking the hard question here.

"I was thinking about kissing you. It just popped into my head." I fidgeted. "I have been struggling with my attraction to you, balanced with my need to get to know you before getting too involved."

She said she was impressed with my honesty and was struggling with the same thing. She leaned over and kissed me. It was a short, soft kiss on the lips, followed by another open, longer kiss. I let myself go into it. This time, I let out a little moan.

She then backed up a little and looked at me.

"Let's not let the physical stuff take us over here. At least we know there is chemistry."

I felt a great sense of relief. She got up and made a fresh pot of coffee and some sandwiches. We ate picnic style in the middle of the living room. We spent the rest of the afternoon learning about each other. She played sports throughout high school and softball in college. She picked psychology because she enjoyed the study and had never tired of it. She found private practice satisfying but enjoyed seeing the little lightbulb go on for students when she introduced them to new ideas.

I told her my coming out story. I shared that I remember loving women since my earliest memories. I told her about all of my various crushes on teachers, student teachers, coaches, and camp counselors throughout my life. "My first love was also at age seventeen. I had fallen in love with my best friend. We had played softball together since the age of six in summer league. She went to the private high school in town, while I went to the public school. She was an only child and doted on by her parents.

"We didn't realize we were falling in love until we were at a party. She lived in a mansion in Congdon. Her parents had gone out of the country on a work trip, and we invited our friends from both schools over. We all drank too much. Played the usual drinking games of quarters and spin the bottle. Several kids got sick. No one stayed overnight but me. We ended the night in her bed.

"I think the alcohol allowed us to act on the feelings we had had for each other for a long time. In the morning, we talked about it, asking each other, 'Are we gay?' We didn't really know, but we couldn't stay away from each other. We both ended up going to college locally so we could be together.

"Her parents were not pleased because they had visions of an Ivy League school for their little girl. I came out to my mom and dad in my freshman year of college. She came out to her parents because they caught us in bed. Her mom walked in one morning to get her laundry, and we were naked, sleeping in each other's arms. Her mom sent her to therapy and pressured her not to see me.

"We continued to see each other on the sly for nearly two years after that. I got tired of sneaking and dreamed of an open relationship. I was developing a close-knit group of friends in college who were lesbians, and she couldn't or wouldn't join us. I ended it in my junior year."

The afternoon was winding down. I looked out the window and was alarmed by the amount of snow. It was so high it was making its way up the house to the level of the windowsill. I thought we should try the door, which opened out. We struggled against the weight of the snow and eventually got it open. We both vowed to regularly open it so that we wouldn't get trapped. I suppose we could have made our way out a window. This was some snow.

Zoey went into the kitchen to sort her way through the cabinets and fridge to come up with ingredients for dinner. We settled on broiled salmon, a salad, and garlic bread. Over dinner, she talked about finding her house. She was renting it from the person who previously had her job. Even though the rent was high, it was perfect for her, especially since it was so close to work. Until now, she hadn't known how winter driving would go. She walked to work every day even in the rain, since it was only six blocks away. In her last job, the faculty parking had been six blocks from her office.

After dinner, we did dishes to Melissa Etheridge. Zoey let herself go into the music, allowing herself to sing along this time. I found myself thinking about that kiss. Just as I did, she kissed me again. She pinned me against the sink, put her hand behind my head—not so gently this time—and kissed me. It wasn't the kind of kiss that said hello, or good-bye. It was the kind of kiss that lets off steam and builds more. She backed away, straightened her hair, and asked me if I wanted to watch the other movie. I exhaled deeply, blinked twice, and said "What?" She took me by the hand and led me upstairs to the TV/ bedroom.

Just as we put the other movie in, the phone rang. Zoey handed it to me. It was Lou. He was curious about who was answering my cell. I told him I had forwarded it, and he let it go. Nothing going on with him, he just called to see if anything was up with the case. I told him no. He talked about the view from his hot tub suite on the top floor of the Radisson. I almost envied him.

Like Water for Chocolate was excellent, even though I was watching it for the second time. There are just certain movies I can watch over and over again, and this was one of them. When it was over, we hung out on the bed. I took the lead this time and leaned in for a kiss. I wanted her. I wanted her to want me. I stopped and asked her, "How are you?"

She smiled and looked me in the eyes. "I'm good. This feels right."

She kneeled, straddled me, and took her shirt off. She was wearing a sports bra. She took that off, too. She had full, round breasts. I cupped each one with my hands and gently caressed them. I wrestled her under me, straddled her, and took my own shirt off. I then eased down to within an inch of her. Our breasts nearly touched. She arched so that we made contact. I lowered myself onto her. We spent an eternity exploring each other and caressing each other before I began to work on her pants. She was wearing jeans, and I deliberately took my time getting the snap open. I took even longer with the zipper. By the time I had her pants off, she had let out a little whimper. She didn't take any time at all with my pants. I caressed her through her underpants. She was as wet as I was. I tucked my finger around and under the elastic band in an attempt to tease her just a little more. She let out more than a whimper now, and grabbed my hand. I said, "OK, OK." We spent the rest of the night exploring each other's likes.

Chapter 17

WHEN I AWOKE at 9 A.M., Zoey was next to me, still naked, with a delicious little smile on her face and a cup of coffee for me.

We hung out drinking coffee in bed for a little while. All she had to do was give me that look of amusement, and I wanted her again. This should have been exhausting, but I was cranked. I felt like I had a little motor in me that just kept revving over and over again. We experimented with all of the power dynamics, the boundaries of exploration, and our openness. We learned how to communicate in bed. It was quite a morning.

We finally made it downstairs at one in the afternoon. Starved. I had no bearings. I had to look at the calendar to figure out the day. When we finally did eat, the taste sensation was amazing. We parked ourselves on the floor of the living room again with our backs to the couch. The sensate parts of my brain were lit up like a Christmas tree. I also had a perma grin. I laid my head back and let myself process all of this. This was good. I was worried in the back of my mind about being blinded by sex, but I had given in and over to it. In past relationships when the sex was good, I had worked harder on the relationship issues. This sex was incredible. I could work through a lot. I also felt that we were doing more than just sleeping together. We were listening, communicating. Feeling. In my mind, I was relating it to dancing. I can often tell how well a woman is able to connect with others by how well she can dance with me. How much she can let go without focusing on insecurities or how she looks, just letting the dance move her. I realized Zoey was watching me. She said, "Tell me."

I told her what I was thinking. Without words, she got up, put some Macy Gray on the CD player, and held her hand out for us to dance. She was fearless. I'll never forget that dance. She went right there with me again.

It was now Sunday, and the snow was still coming down. The news put the snowfall at two and one-half feet in town. The previous record for one storm was thirty-four inches. I had a feeling we were going to surpass that. When I was a child growing up in the East End of Duluth, we had a huge snowstorm like this. When it was all over, we jumped off the neighbor's garage into the snow banks for fun. We also ran around the whole neighborhood shoveling out the seniors. I wondered if that still happened with kids today. I really was out of touch with non-delinquent youth and families.

We ventured out again to see how much snow there was. Our little snow tunnel had not completely filled in. We had situated the holes so that the wind was hitting the mound broadside. We crawled into our respective ends and began making the tunnel higher and wider. We spent some time enacting my little fantasy of kissing her warm mouth in the cold. It was better than I had dreamed. I decided that I should share all of my fantasies with her.

We spent the rest of Sunday getting to know each other. We talked of work, our upbringing, values, past relationships, and fears. Significant in Zoey's life was her struggle to finish her Ph.D. She had been working part time and living partially off of student loans. Her academic work was good, and she found the study fulfilling, but she had been in a troubled relationship. Her partner at the time was also going to school. They had little time to be together, and when they were together, they spent most of the time arguing. Her partner ended up having an affair with an undergraduate student. Zoey found out about it in the end stages of trying to complete her dissertation. She struggled through the paper and ended up turning in the last draft in the final seconds of the due date. She actually had to stop her professor from locking the door to his office to give it to him. When it was all over, she stayed in for a week, alternating between the joy of completing her dissertation, anger at her now former partner, and sadness about losing her.

We ended up talking well into the night, and we finally got up on Monday at 11 A.M. The snow was letting up. We ventured out with shovels in hand. The snowplows were nowhere in sight, and well over three feet of snow was on the ground. We shoveled for two hours straight before heading in for a break. We had only shoveled out her small driveway and the front walk. My car and the rear sidewalk were left to be liberated. It took another hour to clear them. The snowplow finally came by at 6 P.M. News reports conveyed which roads had been cleared. The alleyways and some of the small avenues would not be cleared for days. The news stories included segments on kids sliding down the middle of main streets and of daring and near tragic rescues. One woman with only wood heat couldn't get her door open to get to her wood supply and had to burn furniture to keep warm.

I called Kathy and Donna.

"So how was your date?" I asked them before they could get the same question out. Kathy didn't answer me but simply said, "You tell me."

"We're having one heck of a first date."

"Have you slept together yet?"

"Things are going well. Very well."

"Very well?" Kathy repeated.

"I'm not giving you a play-by-play. Are the roads plowed?"

"The highway is, but our road isn't. We can't tell if the Valley Road is or not." Kathy paused, and I could hear muffled talking in the background.

"Donna wants to talk to Zoey."

I handed the phone over. All I heard was, "Uh-huh. Yes. Oh, yes!"

I went upstairs to shower and to give her some privacy. My clothes were in the dryer, and I would likely be back at work the following day. I found myself feeling a little sad about this. I would miss Zoey. I took a long shower and let it all sink in.

Chapter 18

WHEN I WALKED downstairs, she was just hanging up the phone. Immediately after she put down the receiver, it rang again. She assumed it was Donna calling back and said into the mouthpiece, "I'm not giving you the details!"

She got a shocked look on her face, turned pale, and said, "Who is this? Tell me who this is right now!" She gently put the receiver in its cradle, and looked at me.

"What?"

"Someone just threatened to kill me. Or, more likely, threatened to kill you. Do you still have your cell phone forwarded to this number?"

I walked over to her and took her hand. It was ice-cold. I guided her down to the floor. "Yes. What exactly did they say?"

"He said, 'You fucking dyke bitch! You're dead. If Nickel doesn't get out, you're dead. Make it happen.' That's it. I just hung up the phone."

"It was just a kid making a threat. Probably nothing to worry about. Are you OK?"

"Yeah, I'm OK, but how did he get your cell number? Does he have my number now?"

"No, he doesn't. But do you have caller I.D.?"

"I don't think so."

I tried *69 with no luck. I realized that much of the world never needed it. It did come in handy when trying to track down threats.

I called Nate's number, and he picked up. I told him about the call. He didn't know how they had gotten my cell number. It was possible they had taken one of my business cards from my office. He would call Lou to see if he had had a similar threat.

My thoughts raced. Why would they still be focusing on probation? We did get the police into Latrell's place. That must be it. Or this could be related to Nichols's original threat to Lou and me. I hoped Char wasn't being harassed. I pulled out my Palm Pilot, retrieved her home number, and called her.

"Hello."

"Char?"

"Who is calling?"

"Jo Spence."

"Thank god it's you. I just had a scary phone call."

"Me, too. Tell me what they said."

"Some guy basically said, 'Let Nickel and the boys out, or you're dead.' He swore a bit and tried to sound tough."

"Do you have caller I.D.?"

"Yes, but it came through as an unknown caller."

"Shit! Are you OK?"

"Yes—it's not my first threat, but it has been a while since anyone has called me at home. I had my number changed a while back."

I didn't say it but thought that the information must have been gained from the break-in. What did the little bastards do--write down all of the staff names, addresses, and phone numbers? I still wished I knew who had broken into my office, and how they had gained access without any sign of forced entry. I felt I had let the staff down somehow. I gave Nate's cell number to Char and asked her to brief him. I updated Zoey, and we sat there in silence for a while.

Nate called me back after ten minutes. He had assigned squads to run by Zoey's and Charlene's houses periodically. Lou had not received a call, but he was not at home. Nate hadn't been called either. I theorized that the caller only had the numbers from my office. It also occurred to me that the gang knew Nate would be armed and considered him a less vulnerable target. Nate didn't ask about the address I had given him. I was grateful for that.

The call definitely put a damper on the evening. I called D. and K. They agreed to watch my boys for another night. I would stay over and go to work in the morning. Zoey seemed glad for more time, too.

Chapter 19

THAT NIGHT, I had another vivid dream. Zoey and I were skiing on the trail behind my house, heading for the river. It was a gray day, barely light enough for us to see the trail. Three foxes jumped out in front of us. They were small and hungry looking. One of them had a significant limp, and his back leg was withered.

They should not have been that close to us. They circled around us and then morphed into human-like creatures. They had faces and a trunk, but maintained fox ears, tails, and legs.

The leader said, "If we don't get Nickel back, we will kill you."

I felt an inner calm. No threat. I just kept following the trail to finish our ski.

The fox-humans morphed back to foxes and started growling fiercely, running around in circles. One of them took a bite at my calf. I noticed that it was bleeding, but I didn't feel any pain.

Again, I kept skiing ahead with the same inner calm.

Then I woke up.

I went downstairs and found myself cleaning Zoey's kitchen. This was weird, I knew, but I couldn't stop myself. I had all the burner covers off and was scrubbing them with Soft Scrub when Zoey cleared her throat behind me.

"I'm sorry; I clean when I'm stressed. This case is getting to me. I just had a really strange dream."

"Tell me about it."

"Can I finish this first? It helps me to relax."

She gestured with her hand and said, "Have at it."

When I was done, we moved into the living room to sit in front of the fire. I told her the dream in its entirety.

"I have some knowledge of dream analysis," Zoey told me. "Do you want me to help you interpret yours?"

"Yeah, OK." And thought, _what could it hurt?_

"What I think doesn't matter. I cannot interpret your dream for you. What I can do is help you identify your associations to the characters in your dream. Then you interpret it. OK?"

"OK." I said again.

"What does a gray sky mean to you? What feelings does it evoke?"

"Sadness, despair, quiet, calm. All of those things."

"What was the first thing that popped into your mind about the gray sky?"

"Foreshadowing." I said it without thinking, but I knew it was really true.

"Good. Now tell me what a fox means to you."

"Predator."

"Tell me why you thought the foxes looked hungry."

"There was a caved-in look about them. Their ribs were showing. They had a hungry look in their eyes."

"Tell me about the withered leg."

"It was the back right leg. It wasn't functioning."

She interrupted, "Tell me what you meant by 'withered.'"

"Flesh and bone, thinner. It was just this withered thing hanging there. It didn't move with the other legs. It was smaller than the other three."

"How did you know which fox was the leader?"

"It was clear. The leader was out front. The others looked to him. He spoke for the group."

"Were there any additional characteristics about him?"

"Only once he morphed. Then he seemed more puffed up--like he was bolstering himself. The others just watched."

"Tell me about your reactions in the dream."

"I was calm in the dream—even when the fox bit me. I realized that he had bitten me, and I saw blood, but I didn't feel a thing. No pain."

"Now, what do you make of that?" Zoey looked at me expectantly.

"Well, I downplay the risk to myself in this investigation to protect those in my life who care about me. I see the gangsters as kids trying to bolster themselves to have power. I wonder if I might be misjudging these people or this situation."

"Given that, what does this dream mean to you?"

"Even though one fox has a withered leg and is hungry, and the leader is bolstering himself, they are still dangerous."

"What else are you getting out of the dream?"

"I think that it means that everything that has happened all comes back to me. They broke into my office, stole the addresses and phone numbers of my staff. Now those staff members are in danger. This gang came to my neighborhood in the Valley. The entire Valley will never have the same sense of security. My neighbors will all lock their doors now. It's all because of me and my job."

"Whoa! Hold up a minute. How did you bring them into the Valley?"

"Because of my job. Because they came there after me."

"So, you caused them to come out to the Valley?"

"Well, not really, but everyone in my life is at some risk of having contact with these thugs. If we don't round up this gang, the whole city will change."

"And you see that as your job?"

"To some degree. I mean, I have to do my part."

"Are you always this responsible?" I just looked at her. "Does it ever get you into trouble?"

"Is this still dream analysis, where I do all of the analysis?" I asked.

She just laughed at me, lifted her eyebrows, and changed the subject. "Can you go back to sleep?"

"I think I'll just head to work," I said.

She got up with me, and we had coffee and toast. When it came time to leave, I felt a little sad. I had grown accustomed to her company. I couldn't remember the last time I had spent three-plus days with another human being. We kissed, wished each other a good day, and I left.

Chapter 20

THE MAIN ROADS to the office were clear. Even the parking lot of my building was plowed, and the snow banks were huge. In the winter, fewer parking permits are sold to allow for the snow banks, but the property owners still make a mint from the parking fees.

Inside, the building temp was around fifty degrees. I could almost see my breath. It was 6:15 A.M., and there wasn't a soul in sight. I guessed that the building manager would arrive at 7:30 to start up the heating system. Thank goodness for the portable heater under my desk.

No one was around, and I relished the time in my office, making it through the huge pile of paperwork that had been accumulating. Jeannie had been moving documents from my mailbox as it became full, transferring them to my desk. I read and signed predisposition investigations, reference studies, progress and discharge reports, and tossed out all of the junk mail produced by possible referral sources for juvenile out-of-home placements. When I reached the end of the pile, it was eight o'clock.

The office was filling up with employees, but it hadn't warmed up. Most of the staff were sitting at their desks clearing voice mail with their winter jackets still on. I vowed to complain to building management about this.

I took a few minutes to catch up with the front office staff, and did a visual check of the schedule to see who was working where. Tuesdays are usually juvenile court day, but I predicted this day was going to be unique. I doubted that the PD had been mobile enough to make any arrests during the storm, so the only cases would be trials and probation violations. I checked the detention list, noting that the Detention Center was two over their maximum. I would have to remember to call and get the scoop on how

103

they staffed that during the storm. I wondered who the poor souls were who started their shift Friday night. How Warren was coping with the night shift in the Intensive Unit was also on my mind.

Lou and Char gladly joined me in my heated office for a powwow. Lou said he heard that the judge who presided over the decision about the transfer of Nichols from Juvenile Detention to the jail also got a threat. Char said she had had no other problems, and in fact a squad had kept an eye on her house all night. Lou refrained from bragging about his Jacuzzi suite view of the storm. We called Nate, who had nothing new to report. He would keep us posted. I wondered when the sting designed to flush out the leak would go down. I couldn't imagine what they had planned. I wished I could be a part of that.

We all got back to the normal day-to-day office functioning. Nate said he would call Lou if he needed him. For now, it was a waiting game. The men and one boy we got out of the East Hillside house would be arraigned today. Char would cover that hearing and update the judge for bail consideration. I called the county attorney to make sure she knew the tie to the gang and possibly to the Toivunen murders so that she would request high bail. Latrell would be held on a no-bail violation of probation along with the new charges. No bail is customary on offenders with serious offenses who violate probation. The law allows it in only a couple of other circumstances such as murder or when the offender poses a serious imminent threat to public safety. I hate that "presumed innocent" thing. I would make a terrible juror.

At 10:30, I got a call from Nate. He didn't have much, but I thanked him for keeping me posted.

"We're still hoping to get another tip on Smithy Nichols. He is still at large. He likely has some minions working with him. I'm pretty sure he is their gun guy. That's Lou's take, anyway. The local news stations have been flashing his picture everywhere. If he goes out, we'll get him."

After hanging up, I called the security agency that was installing my system. Having to think about security all of the time was really starting to piss me off. Being away from home and away from my dogs was also irritating me. When the receptionist answered, I got myself in check. The system would be in Wednesday. I agreed to meet with the installer in the morning. I could make it one more night. I kind of looked forward to talking to D. and K. about my first date.

Following court, Char reported back that Latrell was held without bail. The other men had bail set at $500,000 each. That was good. Unless they had a huge store of cash lying around, they weren't going anywhere, either. Many drug dealers did have access to large amounts of cash. The primary purpose of bail is to ensure appearance at court. If the defendant doesn't appear, he or she loses the bail. Five hundred thousand would be a lot to lose. Even for a drug dealer.

Bail does not insure public safety. An alleged criminal can post bond just by finding a bondsman willing to write a bond that big. A bond is usually bought for ten percent of the total bail amount. It has to be secured by some real property. If the defendant doesn't show for court, the bondsman gets the assets used to secure the debt. Odds are they don't have legitimate assets.

The juvenile was held in detention. He had no absolute right to bail. By my thinking, this is a much saner system.

At the end of the day, I was beat. I called Kathy and offered to pick up groceries. She gratefully accepted, as their fridge was empty following the storm, and she provided me with a list. I picked up three quarts of ice cream on my own.

Their place was clear of snow. They have a four-wheeler with a snow thrower on the front. I think Kathy loves to ride around on that thing. I had yet to dig out at my place.

We made homemade pizza for dinner. Kathy and Donna were relentless in their quest for details about Zoey and me. While I didn't give them specifics, I did indicate that there was chemistry. Donna talked at length about how good it was to see me with someone who had her life together, not some "granola head." I never realized how she had felt about Dar. I asked her, "So why do you think Zoey and I will be compatible?"

"You're both bright, energetic, and adventurous, but you are different enough to complement each other. She loves the outdoors, and so do you. She is into her work, and so are you; and well, I just thought you would look good together. You just look like you would make a couple."

I was surprised by the fact that Donna saw me as bright, high energy, and adventurous. I laughed out loud about the "look good together" concept. "That's real scientific, isn't it?" I hugged her, and she just smiled up at me. At just slightly over five feet tall, she is just so huggable.

My dogs were at first overjoyed to see me. They ran up to me and licked me anywhere they could. Cocoa howled and talked at length. Then they both tried to ignore me. They were determined to give me the silent treatment. I always find that funny. At some point, they forgave me for the unexcused absence and demanded to be adored again.

After dinner, Kathy and I went to my house and shoveled our brains out. There really was a lot of snow. It took two hours to finish the little garage apron and two sidewalks. Normally, when you shovel, you scoop the fallen snow up into one shovel load and work your way forward down the sidewalk. With this much snow, it took three or four shovel loads to get from the top of the pile down to the sidewalk. The exercise felt good. I contemplated staying at my house but decided that waiting for the security system made some sense.

Back at Kathy's, I called Zoey. She filled me in on her day. She proudly told her coworkers and students about her donut driving and snow angel making. They were unimpressed. She listened to the details of my day, and we made a dinner date for the next night at my house. A moment of uncomfortable silence followed. This is when you tell a lover that you love them. I told her I missed her, and we hung up. I wasn't going to think about this. It was too soon for love. Lust, yes. Like, yes. But love?

Chapter 21

I woke the next morning at 5:58. Back on schedule. Weird. I had time before meeting the security company, so I took the pups out for a walk, using Kathy's huge snowshoes. She would definitely thank me for tracking her trails. With over three feet of fresh snow, the going was slow. The dogs thought they had to lead the way, and they had to jump the whole way. After an hour, they were clearly as exhausted as I was.

Midway down the trail, my mind began to wander to Zoey. I imagined driving up to my house and finding her car already in the driveway. There were lights on in my house. I walked inside. Zoey was nowhere in sight. I walked back to my bedroom. She had my robe on and nothing else. She was holding my handcuffs. Raising them into view, she asked, "Do you only use these for work?"

She had a "dare you" grin on her face. I didn't speak, but walked over to her, took the handcuffs, and secured her to the bed. I then began to tease her slowly. When she got to the point of pleading with me to take her, I stood back, saying, "Oh, I'll take you all right."

That was the end of the fantasy. After the dogs and I got back to Kathy and Donna's, I enjoyed a long hot shower and headed over to meet the security folks.

While they were installing the system, I took the opportunity to reclaim my house. First I brewed up a pot of coffee. I then called work and told them to call me at home if they needed anything. I connected to my work e-mail from my home computer and completed all of the correspondence I hadn't gotten to the day before. Then I did laundry and made chocolate chip cookies for the two guys working on my house. I think they worked a little harder because of it. I had just snuggled into the couch with Patricia Cornwell's latest novel when my cell phone rang.

It was Nate. "Anything on Smithy Nichols?" I asked. "He is our last big catch, right?"

"According to Lou, he is the guy in charge of keeping the gang in weapons. He steals, buys, sells, or trades them. Lou is out right now working his connections to get information. If anyone can get at his location, Lou can. Most likely Smithy would not sell to local gangs, though, for obvious reasons. The FBI is bringing in some dogs trained to sniff out weapons. I think it's overkill. I mean, you have to be near the weapons for the dogs to catch a scent. We're checking our Computer Aided Database for any weapon thefts. That will take time, but we may put some pieces together that way. Can you ask your PO's to renew their efforts in the community?"

"I'm on it. Thanks for keeping me in the loop here, Nate."

"No problem."

I called Don's cell number. As the most senior PO, he was acting supervisor in my absence. I asked him to talk to the other probation officers about the need to flush out information about Smithy. I also asked him to check in on Warren. He generally likes to work alone, but I prefer for him to have someone there for backup. I'd rather be out in the trenches myself, but I also find it harder to coordinate things from there. I get too focused on the fieldwork to see the big picture. I sent a group e-mail to the juvenile unit asking everyone to prioritize finding information about Smithy.

Just as I was finishing up, Lou called, and gave me a quick update. A guy in West Duluth who owned an upholstery shop had allegedly been increasing his net sales by selling meth. Informants claimed that he also had a large collection of guns and would know who's who in the black market gun trade in Duluth. Lou was going to see if Nate and his team of Feebies would set up a buy, then leverage a deal with the shop owner to get information on Smithy. Lou could set it up himself, but he wanted permission to bring in the FBI for the sting. My radar went up about his motive for asking. He would normally just do it without my knowledge.

"Tell me exactly what you have in mind."

"Nothing, boss. I just think this is going to go somewhere, and I want to be a part of it. I have never seen the Feebies work up close and personal. It could be a great training experience for me."

"OK, but keep me posted. Call me if you need me to come out there."

"Got it."

By the time I hung up with Lou, it was four in the afternoon. Zoey was scheduled to arrive at six.

The installers were just testing the system. They would finish after doing some clean-up and demonstrating the unit for me. The system was activated by disturbance at the doors or any of the windows. I had to turn it off and on in order to enter and leave. If I failed to set the alarm, I would be unprotected. If I entered or exited without disarming it, I would set off the alarm and would have only thirty seconds to disarm it with a code before the police were notified. The call would go right to the cell phone of the township police. If they were unavailable, it would forward to the DPD. There was a huge installation fee, plus a monthly charge. Chances were that once we got the last of this gang, it would not be an issue. By the time these guys got sentenced, they would have a whole host of others to focus their anger at. It was probably overkill. I hoped so, anyway.

Chapter 22

ZOEY ARRIVED RIGHT on time. We had steaks and baked potatoes from the grill. I was a little embarrassed by the frozen veggies, but I hadn't had a chance to get to the store to replenish my supplies. It was good to be home. After dinner, we settled into my living room in front of the fireplace.

The dogs had also settled back into their routine, but Java was having another set of issues. He is a lab mix and very tall, weighing in at about eighty pounds. Put out by Zoey's presence, he kept inserting himself between us. It was really something. He would first sit between us. Then he would put his back to me and his paws on her, and literally push us apart.

Together we came up with a plan to help the poor guy out. I showed her where the treats jar was and suggested that she run my boys through several of their tricks. She had them sit, stay, bark, shake, roll over, etc. Each time, she rewarded them with a treat. She then wrestled with one while I held the other one back. Once the roughhousing was done, we settled back down in front of the fire. Java inserted himself between us but this time didn't try to push. We both petted him for a little bit, and then I told him to scram. He obeyed, but went off pouting. He wouldn't look at us. Dogs are so funny.

After settling in, we talked about both of our days. She had a student in one of her classes who was clearly mentally ill, trying to figure out her own issues by taking psychology courses. Zoey said that while life experiences really can help in the learning process and eventually aid a student in assisting others, some mental illnesses just need medication. The troubled ones ended up coming to her for advice or just plain acting out, so she had to gently, or not so gently, get them help.

This student appeared to be depressed and thankfully could remain in school if she got some medication and therapy. The student seemed to be taking Zoey's advice.

Once we were done with the work updates, Zoey got to her feet, smiled, and said, "I think you forgot that CD you wanted to share with me in your car. Could you go get it please?"

I obediently went out to the car to retrieve the disc. When I returned, Zoey was no where in sight. I put the CD in and wandered back to my bedroom. Zoey was standing in my bedroom holding out my handcuffs, saying, "I found these on top of your bureau. Do you really use them in your work?"

"Uh, sometimes … not often." I could feel heat rising from my neck into my face.

"What's wrong?" She asked. "You're blushing!"

"Nothing…I mean, when I was snowshoeing, I happened to think of you and those at the same time."

She got that fearless look again and said, "Maybe you should show me what you had in mind."

I took them from her and cuffed both of her hands to the bed, using a bandanna to attach the cuffs to the headboard. I then painstakingly began to tease her. When she started to cry out, I touched her. What I love about making love with women is the ability to totally focus on pleasing, and then being pleased. I knew her well enough by then to bring her to the edge of orgasm and then to back off just a little. I held her on the edge for nearly a minute before sending her over the top. It was so exciting to me that I came with her. She hadn't even touched me. I removed the cuffs, and we held each other. Spent. She was able to bring me to climax one more time. It was short and intense due to my heightened level of arousal. She asked me if I was able to accept restraint. I felt a little panicked because I had never tried it before, but I heard myself say, "I'm willing to try."

I asked her if she had fantasies. She said, "I sure the heck am going to start to. How do I do it?"

"I don't know, they just happen. They just pop into my head."

I asked her if she wanted to spend the night. She thanked me and quickly fell asleep.

In the morning, I took the dogs out on the trail with snowshoes for a quick walk while she showered. When I got back, she had a big smile on her face. "You have a great shower. I think I had my first fantasy."

"Tell me."

"Oh, I will, but not now. I have to get ready for work, and I have papers to grade tonight. "Can we get together Friday?"

"Absolutely. Your place or mine?" I asked.

"Here." She kissed me and nearly skipped out the door.

Chapter 23

I LEFT THE DOGS inside the safety of the security system and headed off to work myself. My voice mail had a message from Lou.

"Jo, call me on my cell when you get in. We have some interesting developments with the upholstery shop."

When I called him, he was still rolling out of bed. He had had a late night. The FBI had successfully set up a buy at the shop.

"The owner-operator, Mike West, had a ton of drugs on hand. He gave up information on the black market for guns in exchange for leniency on the drug charges. One guy in particular was looking to get his hands on weapons recently. West said that this guy was asking for semiautomatics and Uzi's. He wanted anything with big firepower. He even asked about a rocket launcher. That takes guts in this day and age. West didn't have anything that big, mostly handguns and high-powered rifles. Chances are he sold him something, but we may never know what. The buyer first called and then came to the shop. He fit Smithy's description. The PD got a warrant to obtain phone records. They should have a location sometime this morning, assuming he didn't make the call from a disposable cell phone."

"Thanks, Lou. I'll wait to hear about progress. I'm going to call the jail to see how things are going there."

Before calling the jail, I put a call into a florist. I ordered a dozen roses of assorted colors and requested that they be sent to Zoey at the university. I wanted to buy all red but for some reason struggled against it. On the card, I asked the florist to write, *You are incredible. I so look forward to Friday. Jo.* The woman who took my order didn't sound uncomfortable at all. I wondered if she had been through diversity training.

The gang members had been put in isolation at the jail. Captain Jolene Greg was still concerned about their safety and would transfer them to another jail as soon as they were arraigned. Nichols was scheduled for a hearing of some sort at 1:30 P.M. in front of Judge Manning. This was some kind of a bail review set up at the request of his public defender. It pissed me off that Nichols had a publicly paid lawyer. He had no documentable income but probably had more cash than my entire staff makes in a week. It just didn't seem right.

I called Nate to update him on the hearing. He said that he would have officers cover it. He also said that he had a possible address for the older Nichols brother. The call to the upholstery shop had come from the Blue Lagoon.

The Lagoon is an apartment building that I can see from my office window. The owner is a convicted sex offender who routinely rents to guys fresh out of prison. The local supervised-release halfway house had developed a working relationship with the guy in order to gain some supervisory contact there. What irks us about this building is that offenders can watch their probation and parole officers come and go from work, and plan their mischief around it. We do like the close proximity, though, because it allows easy office visits for the clients and we can do quick home checks. Every once in a while, I see kids coming in or out of there, and I just cringe. I walk straight down to the parole officers' unit and tell them.

I offered to let the police and feds use my office to set up the bust. Nate accepted. He had been waiting for Lou to grace them with his presence, hoping for just such an offer. The swarm would take place at noon.

Zoey called my office at 10:30, thanking me for the flowers. She also thanked me for the previous night. We purred a little at each other before hanging up. I sat in silence for a minute, letting my emotions wash over me. This was an incredible affair. I wasn't afraid of the intensity, but I was afraid it might not last. I thought about my past long-term relationships and about how the sex dwindled over time. In some cases, it was replaced by a deeper love; in some cases, companionship. I was going to ride this wave for all it was worth. Who knew? Maybe this relationship would last, and we could find a way to keep the passion alive. I realized I had started dreaming about a future with Zoey. That scared me. I did some mental gymnastics around that for a while, and then refocused on work.

The raid happened precisely at noon. The planning for it began at 11:30, and the raid was carefully strategized. Sam Lawson from the FBI coordinated the bust. Sam is the head of the local branch of the FBI in Duluth. Medium height, wiry, and intense, she seemed gay to me. I had never seen her out at any of the social functions, but she did regularly attend the women's university hockey games with another woman.

She first examined the Blue Lagoon on foot and then again from my office window. She drew a diagram of the building and sketched the interior hallways and exits. She assigned each person a location and role. They all had closed-circuit headsets on. I even got one and would watch the entire operation from my office. I was to alert the team to anything I saw that might help. Lou was set up in a hotel room with a view of the opposite side of the building and his own headset.

The officers poured down the stairs and out of the building. Each took his or her assigned position. From the planning meeting, I knew that the building had no security door. The entry team would open the front doorway, traverse one flight of stairs, go down a long hallway, and ram the door of Smithy's apartment. I heard nothing on the headset except scuffling feet until they were in his one-room apartment.

"Entry team in. All secure. Subject is not present. We have found something, though. All parties regroup at probation."

When they came back to the meeting room, I offered them fresh coffee. They laid out what they had found—a diagram of the jail and the Courthouse, and a city map. There was a red line plotting a route from the jail to the Courthouse. It appeared that Smithy was planning to free Nichols.

Lawson quickly called the jail to check on the status of Nichols. He was en route, being brought down to the Courthouse with the afternoon run. The PD had assigned a squad escort. Nate checked in by police radio. They were just leaving the jail. Lou told them to "maintain 20 at the jail." I quickly called Jolene Greg's direct line and briefed her. She instructed me to drive right into the sally port. When we arrived, the van full of prisoners was sitting inside the sally port waiting to exit. Jolene was standing beside the van. Lawson and Jolene talked for a minute. They decided to send all of the prisoners in another van and replace them with FBI agents in the original van. The agents didn't take time to change into jail orange but just poured into the secured van. Lou, Nate, and I trailed from a safe distance in an unmarked squad.

Nate launched into his usual diatribe about arming probation officers, and I looked at him, saying, "Nate, bring it up with the Minnesota Department of Corrections. I am in total agreement with you right now."

Chapter 24

LOU AND I HAD bulletproof vests on. Mine was a lovely green camouflage with pockets for ammunition everywhere. His was plain gray. We trailed the secure van by three quarters of a block. Our vehicle was a tan 1999 Crown Victoria with civilian license plate tabs, and therefore was considered unmarked. I suspected that every bad guy out there could easily identify the unmarked squad cars. I also silently questioned the tactics of having us along at all, but what the heck. It was fun, right? Lou looked at me with a shrug, expressing the same sentiment.

We made the entire trip without incident. At the Courthouse, no sally port awaited us because it was still in the planning stages and had been for nearly a decade. Because the Courthouse is an historic building, the addition would cost a small mint to build so that it would blend in. The prisoner van usually pulls up to the back of the building, and the prisoners file into a door that leads to the holding area. All of the prisoners are shackled and cuffed with belly cuffs. No one can tell the traffic offenders from the felons. The Courthouse also has no secure elevator, so when prisoners are escorted to their hearings, they travel on the same elevator used by the general public. This can make for some interesting elevator rides. I was relaying all of this information to Sam via the headset. All of the officers involved could hear.

She replied with, "Excellent! I knew there was a good reason I asked you to tag along."

Lou gave me a quizzical smile, which I took to mean, "She's a dyke, you're a dyke, interesting?" I could see the wheels turning in his head about where I had been during the storm. I put a silent bet on the fact that he would look into it further. I just shook my head no with a little grin. I'd keep him guessing a bit. I wondered if everyone could tell I was having the best sex of my life. That thought stopped me short. I realized it was true.

We pulled up to the Courthouse a half block back from the secured van with the agents inside. Now what were they going to do? The vehicle with Nichols in it, having taken a separate route, pulled up to the building. The FBI team created a human shield, ushering him into the building. He was now securely inside. Smithy was nowhere in sight. We didn't know the make and model of his vehicle, or whether he even had one.

During the half-hour wait before Nichols's court appearance, we hung out in the holding area. There was a desk in front of three secure holding cells. The prisoners were housed several to a cell while they waited for their court hearings. When the bailiff announced the Nichols hearing, he was transported to his court appearance via the back elevator with a jail deputy and four FBI agents. Nate and I walked up the three flights to Judge Manning's chambers on the fourth floor. The other agents were interspersed throughout the Courthouse. The St. Louis County Sheriff's Department Chief of Security, who was also housed in the Courthouse, had caught up to us and was now coordinating with Sam. They had placed an FBI agent under cover as a prisoner in orange; he was already waiting in the custody box of the courtroom.

Manning's courtroom was identical to all of the courtrooms on the fourth floor of the Courthouse. Each of them was bigger than my entire house, with twenty-five-foot plaster ceilings. The acoustics were horrible, so each courtroom had to be set up with several microphones. I think the basis for retirement for most judges is their inability to hear proceedings. Nichols and the undercover agent were seated together in a four-seat area to the right of Judge Manning's bench. The empty jury box was to the left. The lawyers' tables were nearly directly in front of the judge. There were benches in the back three quarters of the courtroom to accommodate observers. A bailiff sat at a table near the in- custody box.

The bailiffs in the Courthouse are all retired police officers or Courthouse personnel. Many of them are over sixty. They control the flow of people and lawyers, and keep track of who is ready to proceed. They tell you that their job is to throw themselves in front of a bullet heading for their judge, should the need arise. I think they underestimate the speed of the bullets. The bailiffs run the gamut from crotchety, bitter old cops who think offenders are all scum, to extreme extroverts, who love all of the interesting people who come through court. Judge Manning's bailiff is the crotchety old sort.

The Judge was still in chambers, presumably putting on his robe. Some of those robes are pretty scruffy up close. Judge Manning, being one of the more senior judges, must have worn his considerably. I was still contemplating the condition of his robe when he entered the courtroom.

"All rise, District Court is now in session. The Honorable David M. Manning presiding."

Judge Manning stood at his bench and motioned for us to sit with a simple gesture. The younger judges still fluster a bit at the formal gesture of respect.

"Counsel, please tell me why we are here. This matter has already been arraigned."

"Judge, Richard Johnson for the defense. This matter is before you for a bail review. I request a bail reduction."

"Have there been any substantial changes since your client's arraignment?"

"Yes, your honor. There have."

"Any objection from the prosecution?"

"Jon Detarrio for prosecution, your honor. We request the right to respond."

Judge Manning nodded at prosecution and motioned with a hand gesture for the defense to begin. "Let's hear it."

Johnson stood, buttoned his suit, and placed his hands on the table for effect. "Mr. Nichols has been held in isolation for the past week and a half. He is only let out of his cell for an hour of supervised exercise a day. All of his meals are served in isolation. He is innocent until proven guilty, your honor. The isolation is affecting his mental health. He is withdrawn and depressed."

I looked over at the bailiff and saw him roll his eyes. I could just hear him. Oh, poor baby, should we get you cable TV? Would that help your mental health? How about a massage?

"Please advise on why he is in isolation, Mr. Detarrio."

"He is being kept separate from other gang members. Several of his known associates were arrested for attempting to break into the Juvenile Detention Facility by shooting their way in. They were attempting to free Mr. Nichols. If Mr. Nichols has free roam of the jail, he poses a serious threat to the guards and to other inmates. He is provided with reading material and is also within earshot of a guard for conversation."

"Defense would like to be heard, your honor."

"Enlighten me further."

"These are all allegations. There is no direct evidentiary tie to the alleged gang members or to the break-in. My client was at the St. Louis County Jail when this incident occurred. This is all speculation on the part of some very creative police officers."

I glanced at the bailiff. He was red faced with anger now. Judge Manning was easily ignoring him, but he was providing quite a show for the rest of us.

"Mr. Johnson, are you asking for a psychological evaluation?"

Nichols bolted up a little and whispered into Johnson's ear.

"No, we are not, your honor."

"I do not adjust bail in response to security measures at the jail. It is within the discretion of jail administration to segregate prisoners based on risk. I do not find his treatment cruel or inhumane, and I will not overrule my previous bail ruling based on what I have heard here. Bail will remain the same. Anything further?"

"No, your honor," answered the public defender.

"No, your honor, and thank you," chimed in Detarrio.

Chapter 25

A JAILER ESCORTED NICHOLS out of the courtroom. The undercover FBI agent followed. We were getting up to leave when we heard shots. Three shots--boom, boom, pause, boom. The judge ran back into chambers. The bailiff stood there frozen. We then heard what sounded like a scuffle.

Nate quickly ran to the door with his weapon drawn. He put his back to the door and peeked his head around with his weapon out in front of him pointed to the ceiling. He took one hand from the weapon and gestured for us to stay. He whispered into his head unit, "Armed suspect has a hostage."

There were still FBI agents posted throughout the building. Nate continued talking quietly, "Suspect has two in-custody subjects. Suspect has a gun, and Nichols is with him. They are edging their way toward the back north stairwell. Hostage is a federal agent. Transportation officer is down and in need of assistance. Please call an ambulance."

I took out my cell and made a 911 call. I thought about all of the probation staff housed on the same floor. I prayed no one was on a bathroom break or getting a drink of water.

Sam was still in the courtroom. She walked calmly out into the hallway with her gun pointed at the suspect.

"Freeze! Don't move another inch!"

The rest of us crept up and peered around the door. I couldn't stop watching. "That woman has ovaries," I thought aloud.

"Balls, too," came out of Lou's mouth. We had forgotten about our headsets.

I assumed the man with the gun was Smithy. He had backed toward the stairwell and was ten feet from it, directly in front of the elevator. The elevator dinged, the arrow pointing up lit up, and the door opened. Smithy looked up at the light to see about catching a ride and then peered into the elevator car. There was a federal agent in camouflage standing in the car with a shotgun pointed at Smithy and Nichols.

For a second, I thought about the safety of Nichols. I have often heard officers talk about police-assisted suicide. They are referring to when they have to shoot an armed suspect because the offender fails to respond to commands to put down his or her weapon. If an armed offender makes a move toward the officers, they shoot to kill. Instead of having to deal with the emotion connected with taking a life, they call it a police-assisted suicide. They infer that the individual must have wanted to die.

Nichols spoke up now.

"Back off, all of you! We'll kill him. All of you!"

Nichols was still shackled and belly cuffed. He didn't look convincing, but his brother Smithy Nichols did. He had a gun to the head of the orange-clad agent, who amazingly looked calm. The agent in the elevator had pushed a button so that the doors would stay open. This also sounded a loud ringing alarm, adding a sense of urgency to the scene.

"Mike, we can work this out," Sam said calmly. "Listen to me. There is no way out here. The place is crawling with FBI agents. We have the building surrounded. I can help you get out of this alive. You can have your day in court. Walk away from this."

"No! Fucking, no! You back off. I'm going to get out of here or fucking die trying." He exploded his reply. This was not going well. This was not a negotiation. I had forgotten that his name was Mike. Sam really had done her homework.

"Do you want to go out like this? Take your brother down with you? You seem too smart for that to me. Tell me what you need so your people don't get hurt, and my people don't get hurt."

Sam had not lowered her weapon. There were other FBI agents creeping down the south hallway, and one advancing up the stairs. The Nichols brothers were cornered, and the circle was tightening.

The deputy was still in the hallway bleeding through a gunshot wound to his upper shoulder. He was still, but conscious, and was leaning up against the marble wall. Blood was visible on the wall behind him where he had slid to a propped up position after being shot.

Sam began in an authoritative but calm voice "Look, Mike, let's do this respectfully. I'm the only one who can get you out of this. OK? Talk to me. Tell me how I can get you out of here."

"I'll only talk to Lou."

The word "shit" eased out of my mouth in a whispered breath. Lou straightened a bit, looked at me, and said, "I can do this. Let me at it."

I sat there for what seemed like an eternity weighing things. There was no handy equation for this decision. I said, "Your choice." His wife Sara and their two kids crying at his funeral flashed into my mind. I hoped he had the same thought.

He said into the headset, "I'm coming out."

He walked softly into the hallway. All of the guns shifted a bit. It sounded like a drill.

"I'm here, Nickel. It's me, Lou."

Nickel eased a bit, and then he said to Lou, "This is fucking bullshit. Get them out of here, or this guy is going to die."

I heard over the headset, "Tell him that his hostage is a federal agent."

"Nickel, your hostage is an undercover FBI agent. He would see it as his job to die here, and then the cops will kill you. His family would get a double pension. He would be a hero. Any way you look at this, they win. Don't let them win. If you end this, you are in control, and you maintain respect."

Lou was employing his knowledge of gang social rules, speaking to the leader even though his brother held the gun. Everything is about respect with these guys. Everything is about saving face and being in control. The situation could still go either way. I was certain Nickel did not have it in him to back down.

"I can end this, all right." Nichols turned to the uniformed driver of the first van and said, "Straton, you are the one who fucked this up. You were supposed to get me out of here. Do something."

An FBI agent trained his high-powered rifle at the driver's head.

Straton began to shake. "I don't know what he's talking about. The guy is nuts."

Nichols said, "You were paid good money for protection. You chicken shit. You're gonna fry with me. Never trust a dirty cop. You can't turn on me and get away with it. I've got proof. My boys have you on tape."

As Straton made a move for his weapon, an agent shot the gun out of his reach. I was impressed as hell that they didn't shoot him.

At that point, all weapons were trained on Nichols. Lou was twelve feet from him. Smithy and the hostage were to his right. There was a clear shot at Nichols. Smithy's finger was on the trigger, his gun barrel pointed at the hostage's head. Over the headset I heard, "Clear shot at big Nichols." "Clear at Nichols here, too." "Locked on to armed subject."

"Nickel, listen to me." Lou sensed he was running out of time. "Do you trust me?"

"More than the others. You still locked me up. Where is that dyke bitch boss of yours?"

"Listen, I'm not going to screw you. If I hadn't locked you up, you might be dead now. This thing is all messed up. It didn't go like you wanted it to, so back up and try it again. You have leadership skills, man. Going down here will waste all of that. Don't waste all that you have made and become."

There was a long pause. Nichols was wired. He looked like pure potential energy.

"All right, I'm in control here. Do what I say. Smit, lower the gun. Everybody just chill the fuck out! Do you hear me? Chill. Take a pill. It's not time yet to spill." He then walked toward Lou and stood next to him, looking at Smit. I thought to myself, Smit does make a whole lot more sense than a name like Smithy. That just didn't fit for a gangster.

Smit looked at him and put the gun down. The agent who had been held hostage stepped aside and into the elevator. Smit just stood there, dumbstruck. The agents pounced on him, and within seconds, he was on the floor and cuffed. Lou asked if he could escort Nickel to the holding cell. Sam said, "Only with some help."

The paramedics rushed up to the transportation officer. I exhaled as they announced, "He's alive; vitals look good, but he's lost a lot of blood." They worked quickly and had him out of there in less than three minutes. The crime scene was secured, and I took the stairs down to the street. Lou walked up to me outside.

"Nice work, Lou."

"Thanks. I was scared shitless."

"Me, too. I had a vision of your funeral."

"Really?"

"Really."

Chapter 26

WE WALKED OVER to the office. This would elevate Lou's status with the PD and the FBI to hero territory. It might hurt his status as a PO within the juvenile unit though. If he got too much attention because of this, his coworkers could feel threatened by his success. Once back at the office, I took this into consideration when updating the staff.

One PO in particular came to mind as I was pondering the possible negative impact on Lou. Warren Gott, who was filling in for Lou with the intensive unit, had been passed over for a supervisory promotion, and he seemed resentful whenever Lou or any other PO did something outstanding and received praise for it.

From time to time, a PO has had a flat tire in the middle of a field shift. The flats have been amazingly similar in nature. They all have been caused by sidewall slashes. The slashes have been just deep enough to make the tire lose air about ten minutes from the office. One day, after just such an incident happened in ten-degrees-below-zero weather, Warren made a point of taking out his pocketknife and cleaning the blade in a staff meeting. I had no way to tie him to the vandalism directly, but I had my suspicions. Was his standoffish attitude toward the other PO's just a function of his approaching retirement, or did he harbor real hostility toward them? If he had slashed the tires, I wondered what he thought of kids who did property damage crimes. It made me sad that I had to downplay Lou's work to help him avoid negativity from his colleagues.

I took the scenic route home. Deer season would end the coming weekend. I did a celebration dance in my head. I hoped many got away. A house on the upper side of the street had two deer strung up in a tree.

I wondered what tourists thought of this strange practice. I decided to ask Zoey. Funny, how my thoughts were tending to stray in her direction.

At home, I forgot to disarm the alarm system and had to struggle to remember the deactivation code. I got it in time, and then did a quick scan for damage, as my dogs had rarely spent time in the house without me there. I felt the couch and found a warm spot. I didn't find a second warm spot, but I knew that Cocoa was not likely to be a couch potato. I pictured her parked in front of the dining room window on the watch for squirrels and all manner of things she would catch, given the chance.

In the kitchen, I found a torn-open bread bag. The contents were nowhere in sight. I took a look at the dogs, and both appeared guilty. There was no other damage. I was pleased and told them they had earned a walk.

The trail was easygoing where I had previously snowshoed, but painstakingly slow the rest of the way to the river. Once at the river, I pulled out my cell phone and called Kathy. I told her where I was and asked her if she would give me a ride home if I showed up at her house on snowshoes. She agreed and said she would meet me. I saw her about a third of the way up the river between our houses, and we shoed to her house together. All the dogs were along, and it felt like we were running a dogsled team. I loved watching the dogs run in a pack. Along the way, Kathy asked me how things were going with Zoey. I told her in some detail about the snowy weekend and the date at my house. She advised me not to worry about going too fast, "If it lasts, you will have some good memories. If it doesn't, you will, too. It sounds like you're getting to know each other. That's the important thing."

"Are things always that simple and clear for you?" I asked her.

"Other people's problems are. My problems, now that's another story."

She then asked me if I had thought about what went wrong with Dar and if I had any ideas about how to avoid similar problems. I told her that this time I would try to talk about my feelings and to ask the hard questions.

She smiled and nodded, "That, my friend, is a great place to start."

I asked her if she was worried about the fact that Donna had set this whole thing up, or about how Donna would react if things didn't work out.

"Donna will be OK either way. She just wants you to be happy and settled. I think it might make our friendship a little less threatening to her, too."

I stopped in the trail and looked at her. "Is she jealous?"

"No, not really, just insecure at times. I think it's hard for her that my best friend is a woman. With heterosexuals, the rules are clear. She loves our relationship--envies it sometimes. I think she can get worried when she's feeling insecure or when she and I go through a tough time."

"It sounds like she and Zoey are becoming good friends."

"Yes, I'm glad about that. Nice touch on the roses, by the way. I would have gone with all red, though."

"Small world, isn't it?" She had obviously heard about the color.

When we got back to her house, she invited me in for dinner. She also fired up the sauna so that it would be good and hot when we were done eating. The temperature was 160 degrees when the three of us entered. I was only able to stay in for about ten minutes before having to head outside to cool off. I put on beach shoes and stood in the cold. It was eight o'clock, eighteen degrees outside, and the moon was high. Donna came out right after me, but Kathy, hard-core as ever, stayed in for nearly a half hour. We cleaned up with hot water and soap inside the sauna and walked slowly up to the house. We were steaming naked bodies under the moon. What a life. I found myself thinking about sharing this ritual with Zoey.

After my ride home, I curled up in bed with Patricia Cornwell and the phone. I was feeling pleased that the Gangster Mob was in large part behind bars. I suspected there were only small-time players left out on the street. Lou was most likely back in his own house, too. I pictured Zoey correcting papers on the floor in front of her gas fireplace. I hoped she was having trouble concentrating because thoughts of me kept creeping into her consciousness from time to time. I read for an hour before the phone rang.

It was Zoey. I told her about the big progress in the case and about the sauna. She had spent an uneventful day except for the flower delivery, which had produced quite a few questions and reactions around the office. She commented on who was comfortable asking her about them, and who was not. She was out at the college and found it to be a supportive place. She even had a few students who spoke openly to her about the flowers. A baby dyke in class who played on the women's hockey team came to her office for a question after class and smiled big when she saw the roses, asking, "Do I know her?"

"I guess the student body knows I'm a lesbian. She is going to be a little heartbreaker, that one. Angie Moline. She plays first-line right wing. She had a hat trick in the last home series. Tell me you don't know her."

"No, I don't know her. She sounds like she has spunk, though. How goes the paper grading?"

"It's going fine. I'm a little distractible, though."

We confirmed our Friday date at my house, and I tried to get her to confess the fantasy, but she kept me in suspense. I fell asleep dreaming of a sauna with Donna, Kathy, Zoey, and me.

Chapter 27

FRIDAY MORNING STARTED slowly for me. I couldn't get it together to take the dogs out, and they were pissed. I told them they were spoiled. Cocoa refused to be kenneled, and I had to use a treat to lure him. What a little shit. It occurred to me that they had been inside on the couch all day the day before. I knew I should build a ski into my plans with Zoey somehow. It was so nice to have this case winding down. At least the dogs could be outside today. There would be no bread for them to steal.

The ride in to work was uneventful. No dead deer hanging in trees, none on the rooftops of cars with their tongues sticking out. Still there were many vehicles heading up the shore—hunters eager for their last chance to kill. I said a little prayer for the deer that were left.

The office was already bustling when I walked in at eight. I headed directly to my office with a handful of mail, made a fresh single cup of coffee, and settled into my chair. It actually felt good to just sit at my desk. This had been some week and a half. There were no urgent messages on my phone. There was one thank you call from Sam, and another from Jolene at the jail. Nothing from Nate. I called Lou and asked if he could come back to his unit He agreed. Lou didn't think there would be any big gang-related events with the Duluth Gangster Mob. He also had slept at home last night. I asked him if he had any contact with Warren after my public acknowledgment the day before. Lou said he hadn't heard a thing from him. I thanked him for all of his work and encouraged him to take some well-earned time off before being assigned back to the intensive unit. He said he would be ready to go back on Monday.

I called Nate, who was glad to hear that Lou didn't think there would be any more big surprises with the remaining gang members. I asked him if he ever figured out who had broken into my office. He hadn't processed the fingerprints yet but would get to it once he was done filing the police report on Smit. The transportation officer who had been injured in the shooting at the Courthouse was doing OK. Most of the FBI agents had returned to Minneapolis. Because the attempts to break the prisoners out of jail were federally classified offenses, Sam would follow this to the end. She had jurisdiction on any case that would wind up in federal court. Nate thanked me for the help, and we agreed to jointly take Lou out for a high-end dinner.

I called the Chief of Probation to update him. He was relieved to have it over. He also wanted me to write a letter of commendation for Lou's personnel file. I agreed. This thing really was over. I thought to myself, That security system was overkill.

I finished out the day with paperwork and picked up groceries on the way home. I was looking forward to my date with Zoey. She had left me wondering about her fantasy. I liked wondering.

I had time for a quick ski with the dogs before Zoey arrived. They easily kept up with me through the deep snow. They seemed to appreciate the increased speed compared to snowshoeing. Zoey pulled up just as I was skiing back into the yard. I glided up to her car and kissed her through the open window.

"Mmmm … life is good." she said.

"It might get a little better."

"It just keeps getting better and better."

I noticed that she had an overnight bag, and that she was carrying her roses. I placed them on the kitchen breakfast bar. While I prepared dinner, she caught me up on her workday. She had returned the students' papers, pleased with their progress and grades. It was her Introduction to Psychology class that freshmen take to determine their interest in the study of psychology. Asking freshmen to write a paper was stretching it a bit, but she liked to push her students hard. She was also teaching Abnormal Psych and History & Systems—she was opening me up to a whole new world. I loved listening to her talk about her work. I would have had a major crush on her if she had been one of my professors in college.

After dinner, we once again found our way to the floor of the living room in front of the fire. She was sitting between my legs, leaning back against me.

The now familiar scent of her shampoo wafted its way to my nose. I inhaled deeply and asked about her fantasy. She told me that while she was in the shower, she had focused on the sensation of the water and had consciously relaxed her mind. Suddenly, I was in the shower with her.

"I began working soap into a lather in my hands. The water was pounding on me. I rubbed your back, fixated on how the tiny bubbles slowly rolled over your curves. I then moved to the place where your jawline and neck meet just below your ear. Have I mentioned I like that spot? I lathered that area and then allowed my fingers to slide gently over the contours where all of those places come together. It sent a hot shock through me. I turned you sideways. Your eyes were nearly closed, and you were giving yourself to the caresses. I moved lower and lathered each breast, taking special pleasure in the way the water hit your nipple and jumped off slightly. I worked lather into all of the little crevices of your body. I lingered over the back of your knees and the little crease just inside your hip. Have I mentioned I love that spot, too? I took a moment to kiss that spot. Then I took the portable showerhead in my hands, dialed it to pulsate, and slowly worked my way down. I'll have to show you the rest, but you let out quite a scream of pleasure in the end."

I sat there stunned. That was some first fantasy. I was wet. She stood up, took my hand, led me into the bathroom, and showed me the way to a scream of pleasure.

When we were done with water sports, we threw on big flannel shirts and resumed our spot in the sitting spoon position on the floor in front of the fire. Java could not insert himself in this position, so he was quite obviously looking away from us.

We spent the night talking about past relationships and about what went right and wrong with them. I confessed my desire to be more open because while my past relationships were open sexually, they began to fall apart as issues surfaced. Zoey had been in two prior partnerships—one in graduate school and one following. The last one lasted six years. They had bumped along quite happily for four years with relatively little conflict. Although they had never discussed it before, Claire suddenly wanted to get pregnant. Zoey had never thought about having kids because she didn't feel maternal at all. Claire told Zoey that she was running out of time, ended the relationship, and was involved with someone else within two months. For the past two years, Zoey had remained single.

Zoey spent the night. For most of Saturday, she worked on preparing for the following week's lectures. I puttered around the house and finished my Cornwell novel. It was nice to do parallel things while just hanging out in the same space. I called Kathy and Donna, and invited them over for dinner and cards. They suggested their house. I consulted with Zoey, and we compromised on a joint ski to their house followed by dinner. Luckily, Zoey fit into my spare boots. I am not a minimalist when it comes to ski equipment.

She had never been cross-country skiing before, so we started with a practice session in the driveway of my house. It didn't take long for both of us to figure out that she had natural ability.

When Kathy and Donna arrived, we set off with headlamps to light our way. Our snowshoe tracks made for fast skiing, and the snow was dry and clean. The river flows down a three percent downgrade, so the skiing was in large part just gliding and poling. There were a couple of waterfalls along the four-mile route, where we usually tell novices to take their skis off and walk down these steep drop offs. When we reached the first waterfall, Zoey said, "Let me see you guys do it, then I'll decide."

We complied in part. I had Donna and Kathy go first, then Zoey. I wanted to bring up the rear in case of a spill. She made the first hill easily, letting out a "Ya-hoo" in the middle. When I got to the bottom, she planted a big, juicy wet kiss on me, saying, "This is so exciting!"

Donna and Kathy just watched and smiled.

The second waterfall was much bigger. It also ended in a large frozen pond. A family who lives nearby sometimes shovels it for skating. This can be a big surprise for skiers who suddenly run out of snow and traction. We assumed the same order as in the previous waterfall, and Donna actually took a spill at the bottom. They hollered up that the bottom wasn't shoveled. I took a minute to tell Zoey how to fall without breaking her wrists as well as how to snowplow. She informed me that she had done some downhill skiing in the mountains of New Mexico and knew perfectly well how to snowplow. She went for it, making it all the way to the bottom, falling only when I was standing next to her. I pretended to fall, too, and landed right on top of her. We laughed and rolled around a bit, while Donna and Kathy made a dramatic effort to fall on each other, too. The dogs quickly joined in and began licking our faces.

At Kathy and Donna's house, we decided to postpone dinner until after a sauna. The sauna was hot, and we were cold and wet. Zoey couldn't believe we were all getting naked but played along. She was able to stay in as long as Kathy. When she finally did make it out to cool down, she let out a "whoo-eeeee." She was steaming from everywhere. She just stood there cooling down and taking in the feel of being naked in the fifteen-degree air. I encouraged her to stay out until she was actually cold before going in to heat up again. Donna and Kathy cleaned up in warm water inside the sauna and walked into the house without a word. We took our time and played, recreating the water sports of the previous night. By the time we got to the house, we had not cooled down at all.

Over dinner, Kathy shared with us a remodeling plan that she had just created. Her clients were actually friends of mine. I had known Tina in high school and college, and we had played sports together since we were fifteen. I met Sally years later when she got together with Tina. They had purchased a home in the cozy East End neighborhood of Lakeside, had one baby, were looking to have another, and their house was getting tight. One room had been added previously, but it had no real foundation because it was built on posts. The house also had add-on porches in the front and back. Kathy had come up with an ingenious way to expand both porches, thereby creating a three-season room upstairs. She also redesigned the addition so that it was usable as an extra bedroom. The plan expanded the usable closet space both upstairs and downstairs. Kathy would be going over the plans with Tina and Sally the next day. She had printed out plans using a CAD computer program and had digitized several three-dimensional pictures of the plans. Even I could tell what the final product would look like. We were all impressed with how the plan had made the house look more cohesive.

After our late dinner, we all piled into Donna's car and made the trek back to my house for dessert. I broke out the ice cream and made decaf cappuccino.

The night was comfortable, our friendships easy. Zoey seemed to fit in well. I don't think either one of us was nervous. Donna had a perma-grin on her face all night. I was sure that she would take credit for anything good that developed between us. I was more than willing to let her fancy herself a little matchmaker.

Zoey spent one more night, even though she hadn't planned to. On

Sunday, we spent the morning in bed drinking coffee and reading the paper. Both dogs had snuggled in as well. I think we were over the hump with Java. He had begun to see Zoey as part of the pack. I had, too. She made her way home at two in the afternoon.

Chapter 28

AT WORK ON MONDAY morning, I had a message to call Sam ASAP. I returned the call even before making my first cup of coffee.

"We've had an interesting development. Our sting is paying some dividends." I couldn't imagine what could possibly involve me at this point in time.

"What?"

"You have a juvenile PO named Warren Gott?" She knew the answer.

"Yes, why?"

"Well, he attempted to visit the Nichols brothers in jail Saturday. Does he have any interest in this case? Has he been involved in any way?"

"Not that I know of."

"What is he like? I mean, do you have any concerns about him?"

I was on shaky ground here. Personnel matters are confidential. I didn't really have anything on him, either, except speculation and gut feeling. It was, however, a strong gut feeling.

She heard my hesitation and said, "OK then, off the record."

"Well, I have nothing solid on him, just a feeling."

"I'm asking Nate to run those fingerprints from your office right now. Do your PO's get fingerprinted when you hire them?"

"They do now, but Gott was hired twenty-four years ago. The old-timers were not required to be fingerprinted when the policy went into effect so he was grandfathered in. He has no criminal record that I know of. Do you think he's responsible for the break-in?"

"Could be. Let's not jump to conclusions, though. I need you to get his prints somehow, without his knowledge."

"Do you realize what you're asking me to do?"

"Do you want to clear a man who might be wrongly suspected of something very serious?"

"Good point."

"If we get a warrant, his reputation is shit," Sam explained. "And so am I for looking at him. This is the kinder, gentler way."

"OK. I'll get them."

I sat there thinking for a while. She was right, this was the kinder, gentler way. If it was him, I was going to nail his ass to the wall. The thought of him breaking into my office really pissed me off. I let the anger fuel me into action.

My plan was to ask him to meet with me regarding the juvenile work crew and an idea the chief had to turn it into a restorative justice program. He was an old-timer and not likely to question my seeking the advice of someone in the know. I did it all the time. I told him I could only meet at noon and offered to buy lunch. The work crew was a simple program. The crew leaders took court-ordered kids out into the community to do work projects as a consequence, with a general tie to repaying society for the harm caused. The work projects have no real connection to the harm, but rather serve as an abstract reparation. Restorative justice ties the consequence more directly to the crime, and to the victims. The offender has to apologize for the harm and complete a work program that ties as directly as possible to the crime.

I had pizza and pop delivered to the small meeting room. I actually liked the program design I came up with as a ploy and vowed to get someone moving on it in the near future. Warren gave me the expected advice: "Leave it alone! It works fine as it is." I thanked him for his input and offered to clean up. After he left, I grabbed a pencil, picked up his empty can by putting the eraser end into the opening, and dropped it into a brown lunch bag. I then carried the bag straight to Sam's office.

Sam was amazed but not surprised at the speed of my sample collection. I outlined the process, and she was impressed. The pizza oil would help with the prints. She called a lab tech., who promptly collected the specimen. She asked me if I would like to wait while they compared prints. I was happy to. Sam is a very attractive woman who exudes confidence and power. She isn't over the top, though, and seems really secure with herself. I wondered if it helped her in the work she had chosen. Sometimes it is hard for men to accept women in positions of authority, let alone in an agency that is above the Police Department in the hierarchy of law enforcement. I sat there contemplating this, lost in my own thoughts, until I realized she was watching me.

"What on earth are you thinking about?"

"What is it like being a woman and being head of the FBI unit for this city?"

"Truthfully, I don't think about it much. In the early days, I was aware I made some men uncomfortable and suspected that they had a regular comedy routine about me. Over the years, I guess they have come to accept me. They really just want to be treated with respect. I do that. It goes a long way. I also do good work and recognize the good work of my unit. A lesbian with a good work ethic can gain acceptance in the ranks. I think it's much, much harder for gay men."

I didn't acknowledge that she had just come out to me, but I was a bit surprised.

"If you don't mind my asking, are you out to your staff? I mean, do you talk about your partner? Bring her to work functions?"

"Well, that was a long question. No, I don't mind you asking. Yes, I am out in the office. I talk about Sharon when it comes up, but no, I don't bring her to work functions. I don't take her because she has no interest in trying to mingle with that group. It would be cruel and unusual punishment. We do, however, go to dinner or an occasional movie with one of my fellow officers and his wife. It's a little lonely at the top as a lesbian. Honestly, I can't remember anyone ever asking me about it. Thank you. How is it for you?"

"Well, I'm not the big boss, so I think it is a little easier for people to swallow. I try to work hard, and I think you are absolutely right, respect breeds respect in every case. I also try to give people the benefit of the doubt. I treat them as if they can handle it. I think that helps a lot."

"That's a great practice. So, are you seeing anyone, Jo?"

I think I actually blushed, laughed, and said, "Why, what have you heard?"

"Oh, I see. This must be pretty new, and pretty amazing to make you blush. I don't think I have ever seen you blush before."

I gave her the quick rundown on Zoey. She asked me what I liked about her. I had to stop and think about that for a minute. I had never asked myself that question.

"She is bright. Fearless when it comes to trying new things."

She raised her eyebrows at that.

I blushed again.

"She's secure. She asks and answers the hard questions. She's attractive. She's into her work, even passionate about it. She's kind and a good listener. She loves the outdoors."

"And she's single? Well, you go for it. You deserve it. It sounds like you are in love."

I blushed red-hot again. Damn it. There was that question again.

She just smiled at me and said we should go to lunch sometime. It felt good to talk to someone in the field and be open. I agreed. She made a fresh pot of coffee, and we wandered to the lab with cups in hand. The lab technician was in the process of comparing the prints on the computer. He said he had already done a visual, and it was a good solid match. I was instantly pissed.

"How many of Warren's fingerprints did you find on my file cabinet? Are you sure he actually broke into it?"

"It's him, all right. We even lifted prints off of the contents of Lou's file. No doubt about it, he's your guy. It will stand up in court."

"So, where do we go from here? If he did this, there's a better than average chance he's tied to the Gangster Mob."

"I'm glad you see it that way," Sam said. "I want to tie him to it. With his visit to the jail and now this, it's enough for a warrant to search his house and office. I think I could get a judge to go for all bank and phone records, too. I am no longer worried about his or my reputation. We could also just watch him for a while, see what develops."

"I don't want him anywhere near clients." I was still angry. "Who knows what else he's been up to?"

"I understand that, but if the search turns up nothing, all we have on him is breaking and entering. Because it was federally classified confidential data, he can be charged with a felony. That's why it's mine. If he knows we are on to him, he'll lie low."

"What would he have in his house?"

"Anything that ties him to Nichols or the other gang members would make this a crime committed for the benefit of a gang. He would do some real time. Not just probation."

"I'm in favor of that. The sooner we get something on him, the sooner he is away from client contact."

She walked me to the door with a promise to call me for lunch when the case was over. I told her I would love that. I also gave her my cell number so she could call me with the results of the search warrant. With any luck, she would call tonight.

By the time I got back to the office, the workday was over. I took the opportunity to clear my mailbox, voice mail, and answering machine in peace. I also called Lou to check in. He was back working in the intensive unit, and he said he was fine. I didn't tell him about the search warrant or about Warren. I trusted him, but that information was "need to know." He would know soon enough. The intensive unit did carry police radios, but I doubted that the FBI would use them. If things went badly, he would know. Lou was still working the streets and hangouts for information on small-time gang members we had not rounded up yet.

It was six o'clock by the time I finished up. I called Zoey. She was fixing dinner and invited me over. As we settled into dinner, I realized that I was at a loss for words. I was also a little uncomfortable. She asked me what was wrong. I told her I didn't know. She said she would respect that and asked if it was about her. I told her I didn't know that, either. I felt like a heel. Now she was going to think I was having second thoughts. Quite the opposite was true. I was confused by how quickly I was falling in love with her– but I was not at all ready to talk about it. I knew this was not in keeping with my commitment to be more open. I thought maybe I just needed time to process it. When dinner was over, we sat in the living room for a while and just held hands in silence. It was the sweetest thing. I got up to leave and hugged her at length.

I allowed myself to try to process all of it on the ride home. I really do love to drive and think. What I came to was the fact that I didn't have to figure it out. There is no real line about love. It is not an either/or thing. It just is. Even if I was falling in love here, there was much more I needed to learn about Zoey. We had not really had any conflicts yet. How would we handle that? What were her fears? How would they play out in the relationship? We had nothing but time in which to figure all of that out. How the heck was I going to explain this to Zoey? Shit!

An uncomfortable feeling of inadequacy had settled over me. This was the feeling I had lived with for two of the three years with Dar. I didn't call Zoey that night. Instead, I beat myself up about it.

Right after I fell asleep, I dreamed I was in an aquarium full of water. The glass of the aquarium and the water were distorting my images of the outside world. Zoey was looking into the aquarium at me. She was huge. Distorted. I was trying to talk to her, but the sound wouldn't carry. I was naked and wondered what her view of me was from the outside world. I felt both exposed and concerned that the image was wrong. I wanted her to see me for real.

I woke up sweating. I wondered how I could breathe under water. I vowed to talk to her about the issue even if I didn't know how.

I got to work by 7 A.M. after snowshoeing with the dogs for nearly an hour. I peered into Warren's office. I saw no sign of a search. I already knew there was no search because they would have had to call me to gain access after hours. I don't know what made me look.

I called Zoey at 7:15. No answer. I didn't leave a message. Damn, I hoped she hadn't gotten the wrong impression.

At 8:30, I called Sam. She was at her desk.

"I was just about to call you. We executed that warrant last night at Warren's place. He's in custody. We found a stash of rock cocaine and some money. He was also in possession of a 38. That's the same caliber weapon used in the Toivunen family murder. I hope it's nothing, but we're running ballistics for a match. We're still checking his phone records. He had called a tidy little list of gangsters as well as kids. It looks like he was dealing drugs to kids at Central High School."

"Right under my nose!" I was pissed. This far surpassed my anger about him simply breaking into my files.

She allowed me a minute of silence to cool down and collect my thoughts.

"Right under all of our noses. The good news is that this has not been going on long. I doubt he has an offshore account or anything. I think we confiscated his entire stash of dirty money. He had about thirty thousand dollars tucked away in his workshop. He nearly cried when we found it. I do need to get into his office, though. I doubt he has anything in there, but I have to be sure. Can I do that during office hours?"

"Thanks for the courtesy of asking. Yes, you can. The staff will know soon enough anyway. I'll brief them. I need to talk to the Chief. Warren's office was included in the warrant request?"

"Yes, I'll bring it. You OK, Jo?"

"Define OK. I'm pissed as hell. Sad, too. This will reflect badly on some incredible PO's."

"That's how you handle the press release."

"I hadn't thought of that."

I called the Chief, who was on his way over to my office. He and I would address the juvenile staff together. Then he would bring the other units up to speed one by one.

While we updated the staff, Sam and a small crew of crime technicians went through Warren's office. When she was done, she asked to speak to me in private. I escorted her back to my office and made us a fresh brew.

"Jo, I'm going to try and leverage a deal with Warren."

"You can't. He needs to go down for this."

My voice was rising. My face was red.

"I'm not asking."

I sat there staring at her. Incredulous. So much for our new friendship.

"What could you possibly gain from it?"

"We don't know who murdered that family. We need to find justice for that. Nate is actually going to work that angle if we get anything from Warren. We have huge leverage with him. I think we can work a deal that will help to ensure he is not killed in prison. He could do time with white-collar criminals instead of violent criminals. As it is, if he ends up in a standard prison, he's toast. Cops and PO's don't fare well in jail. There are a few who can pull it off if they are big enough, or tough enough. He is neither of those. He's a two-bit slimeball. He would do the same amount of time, but he would get protection."

I breathed a sigh of relief.

"Do you think he knows something? What about the ballistics?"

"Well, the deal will be conditioned on information leading to an arrest. We're still awaiting results on ballistics, but I doubt he's capable of killing four innocent people in cold blood. Whoever killed that family looked them in the eye first. Enjoyed it. I've actually called a profiler from the Minneapolis office to try to get a better idea about who we're looking for. There's a chance we already have him in custody. In the event that we don't, we need to move fast here. Warren has been placed in isolation at the jail for his own protection, but it'll still be hard to protect him."

"Thanks for the heads up, Sam, and let me know if there is anything you need."

"I'll keep you posted."

I sat there thinking about all of this. Would it ever be over? I was actually glad Warren was going to get some protection. He was a slimeball who had disgraced the entire office and abused his authority out of greed, but I thought prison would be justice enough. I don't believe in the death penalty or any type of vigilante justice.

Sam hadn't given me a clue about when they were meeting with Warren, and it irked me a bit. I understood I was too close to it and should not really be involved. But I still felt frustrated. Helpless was more accurate.

I called Zoey. She was not at her desk. I left a message for her to call me back on my cell. I was driving home that night when she called. I asked her if she would meet me at the Lake View Café. She said she would prefer to meet in private. I invited her to my house and told her to make herself comfortable if I was still out skiing with the dogs when she arrived. I was about to explain how she could disarm the security system when she interrupted me and said that she wouldn't be arriving until around seven. When I told her she was welcome to spend the night, she was silent.

Chapter 29

WHEN I GOT HOME, I jumped into my ski boots and hit the trail with the boys. I ruminated about the possibility of Zoey not wanting to spend the night and the possibility that she wanted to end it. All of the bad possibilities kept circling through my mind.

I tripped when one of my ski tips got snagged on a tree branch, and I crashed head first into a snowbank, ending up with a skinned nose. That was going to be attractive. Cocoa and Java offered their slobbery kisses and kept close to me the rest of the way home.

Zoey arrived a little after seven with a wardrobe bag. I hugged her and motioned her into the kitchen. She watched as I made stir-fry. She laughed about my nose. I didn't tell her about my distracting thoughts and felt a little wrench in my gut about not telling her. We settled at the dining room table, which was unusual for us. We usually camped out on the floor.

In my relationship with Dar, when something came up and I didn't talk about it, I found a way to justify it in my mind or minimized it by saying it was all in my imagination. In fact, if I look back on my many relationships, the great divide occurred at around one year. Something would happen, I'd resolve it within my own mind, and one of two other things would occur. I would either settle into a feeling of shame about my inability to risk talking about it, or I would minimize the importance of the problem. Soon I would have several little resentments building. The resentments with Dar were over how we kept the house. They would come out as nagging rather than talking about a possible compromise. I sat there, barely eating, thinking about this.

Zoey said, "Can you tell me what you're thinking so hard about?"

I looked up at her. Those green eyes were fixed on mine. She hadn't said it in a threatening way; instead, there was a slightly curious tone to her voice.

"I was thinking about past relationships and how I didn't communicate. Can we talk about this after dinner, in front of the fire, when I can be touching you?"

She smiled uncertainly and nodded. I picked at my food a little more and fed the rest to the dogs.

Once dinner was over, we settled onto the floor with our backs to the couch. I stalled a little more by building a roaring fire. The house was silent except for the crackling of the logs, which we could hear through the glass fireplace doors. I took her hand. She positioned herself so that she could look into my eyes. I was not used to someone who could be so intimate out of bed. I squirmed a bit, still unable to speak.

She said, "OK, I have an idea. Why don't we dance first? Just try and connect a little."

I put Norah Jones on, cued it to the first song we had ever danced to, and slowly let myself relax into the dance. We moved in unison with no awkwardness. When the song was done, we settled back down to the floor. With the music turned down, I began to tell her what was on my mind.

"I've been thinking about my past relationships and about what went wrong. I didn't talk to my partner about things that were on my mind. I avoided conflict. I had shame about it, which then made it harder to talk."

"Is there something, uh, some conflict between us?"

"No, that's not it at all. I was struggling to put something into words, and then just didn't. Then the whole cycle of shame kicked in. I was afraid you thought I was backing out of the relationship somehow or something else that wasn't true."

"I was a little concerned last night. You seemed distant. Absorbed in your own thoughts. Do you have words yet?"

"I think in part it has to do with my inability to let go with you. I don't mean sexually; that's easy for us. I mean with the rest of it. It's not you. I just can't quantify my feelings for you. We have this incredible physical relationship. I'm so comfortable with you in so many ways, and yet we have so much more to learn about each other." I gestured with my arms out for emphasis. "I also don't trust my intuition about intimate relationships. I feel so blind sometimes. It's like I'm navigating without a compass.

"Someone asked me the other day if I was in love, and I blushed beet red. It caught me off guard. I think I was having difficulty sorting it all out. Then I thought, I don't have to figure this out. We have time. It is what it is. It's also like going to bed without setting the alarm, trusting that things will happen at the right time."

She softened, and touched my hand. "Yes, I agree. Let's take our time. Savor it. If this relationship lasts, we only get one chance to fall in love for the first time. There is no right or wrong. I'm quite happy with things."

"Me, too."

She kissed me. We went to bed early and explored gentle lovemaking. The gentleness brought me to tears. They were not tears of joy or hurt but caused by the depth of emotion I was feeling. I felt like she knew me. I had never felt that with a partner. I also had not realized it was missing before.

Chapter 30

ON MY DRIVE TO work, I basked in a feeling of well-being—a feeling of deep relaxation and contentment I was able to notice the incredible beauty of the lake shore drive.

Unfortunately, work quickly brought me back down to earth. I called Sam first thing. It kind of irked me that she hadn't called me. She wasn't at her desk, so I tried her cell.

"Persistent little bugger, aren't you?"

"Bugger? Well, bugger me with some information about Warren, please."

"I'm just leaving the jail. I'm not at a place where I can talk. Can you and Nate meet me?"

"Sure, I'll set it up. Ground Under?"

"Fine."

"When?"

"Now."

I called Nate. He was out and about and beat me there. They were talking softly at a table in the back. I got a latte before joining them. They stopped talking abruptly when I neared. I did not like suddenly being on the outside of this. What did they think? That I had some undying loyalty to Warren? The news coverage had been brutal. My staff would suffer the ill effects of this for years. There was no loyalty to Warren.

"So, how did the interview with Warren go?"

"Well! Extremely well. I was just updating Nate. This will be his ballgame from now on. I will provide support in any way I can. If this pans out, Warren will have his guarantee of safety. He said that there is one big player out there we haven't apprehended yet, and that this individual is responsible for pulling the trigger on the Toivunens. He said it's a guy going by the name of Richard Rapinski, a.k.a. Rap, a.k.a. Tre. Tre is his most recent alias. Warren doesn't know where he lives, but he hangs out at the Nosy Bar to drink, and shoots pool at the Slam. He is the major muscle for the G.M. Warren described him as a short guy who primarily uses guns to inflict harm. He has a rep for toying with people to scare the crap out of them. He has a total short man complex. He drives around in a jacked-up truck with mud wheels. The name Tre came up because prior to this he had allegedly killed three people. I guess now it's seven."

"I hope this information is good. Did you get out of Warren how he got tangled up in all of this? I mean, I always knew the guy was a bubble off, but this is extreme."

"We asked him that. He said that he got in deep with gambling debt. He hadn't mortgaged his house, but he did borrow money from Nichols. Rather than get his legs broken, he agreed to work for them. He wouldn't say specifically doing what, but we don't think it was limited to peddling dope to kids. You'll be happy to know that he doesn't appear to be working with anyone else in your department."

"So what were you talking about when I walked up?"

"We were talking about a bad cop."

"It's not fun, is it?"

"Good to clean the rats out," said Nate.

"What's next?"

"Run down Tre," Sam responded. "We don't want your folks messed up in this at all. The guy is armed to the teeth and likely escalating in his need to kill. I'm going to feed what information I have about him to our profiler to see if there is a best way to approach him. What your office can do is to call Nate with any leads. Please make it clear that your officers are to steer clear of him."

"Understood."

I allowed myself to sit there absorbing things for only a minute. I wanted to have another cup of coffee and weigh how much to tell the staff, but I knew that if they didn't get accurate information from me, they would succumb to gossip. I'd rather give it to them straight than have to clean up a mess of rumors.

When I went back to the office, I called the staff together to discuss the news coverage about Warren and how it was affecting them. I also called the agency that does our critical incident debriefings. This would affect every person in my unit. I wondered if the agency had ever facilitated a debriefing with such a large number. We scheduled it for noon. I ordered pizza.

I couldn't stand the wait before the staff debriefing, so I deep-cleaned the staff kitchen and lounge. I think I am the only one who ever does it, and it needed it. The sink had a layer of scum, the coffeepot was stained black, and there were dishes to scrub. I pushed up my sleeves and dug in. I spent an entire hour scouring and scrubbing. Don walked by, smiled, and said, "Stressed out? Well, something good may come of this after all."

For Christmas, I often get cleaning supplies from an anonymous member of my staff. I bet most units joke about how their bosses dress, or walk, or something. I'm sure they have anal retentive jokes about me. I just needed some order. I needed to accomplish something.

The debriefing was hard. The juvenile probation officers were angry with Warren for being such a slime. They were angry that the public now associated probation officers with gang-affiliated drug dealing. They were also mad at themselves for failing to see his slide to the dark side. I suspected they were angry with me for not seeing it, too, although they didn't say that directly. All in all, it was a good start. The facilitator encouraged us to keep talking about it and to seek counseling when needed. This issue would be with us for a long time.

Afterward, I kept my staff together to set limits about contact and proximity to Tre. While we could do some nosing around to try and pin down his location, it was imperative not to get labeled as a target, or to draw his suspicion to the fact that we were zeroing in on him, causing him to go underground.

Once back in my office, I called Nate to see if the police had confirmed Tre's full name so that we could see if he was in the probation system. We track all known associates, as well as last known addresses. He informed me that Richard Rapinski was an alias for sure. They had another name, but they were not sure of its reliability. They didn't have enough for a warrant, and they didn't have a known address, anyway. The suspect's name was John Alexander Drift, d.o.b. 5/25/84. That put him at nineteen. That was young for a serial killer. Sam was going to have trouble with that in the profile. While Nate was on the phone, I pulled up our client tracking system. John Alexander Drift was not listed. There were too many Drifts to make any logical connections.

I couldn't run him in the FBI database without an open file, so I checked the Statewide Supervision System. Bingo, we got a match. I could hear Nate's breathing change a bit as he heard this. Drift had picked up a driving-without-a-license charge in Minneapolis earlier in the year. Bless their little hearts for taking the time to enter the data. This was a small-time charge.

There was a picture. He was an ugly little wiry guy, with big ears and stringy blondish hair that hung nearly into his eyes. I asked Nate if he had registered for a link to the Statewide Supervision System, but he hadn't. I scolded him and sent him a link via e-mail. I knew his department had access but gave him my password to save him time. I also printed Tre's picture and distributed it to all the PO mailboxes, sending a note to all of the other unit supervisors to relay the warnings of dangerousness. I called it a day.

Chapter 31

ON THE WAY HOME, I stopped for gas and picked up a gas-station-quality brew. It actually wasn't that bad, but I added cream and sugar for good measure. I took the scenic route and found myself pulling over at Brighton Beach.

Brighton Beach is a one-mile park that contours Lake Superior jutting off from the North Shore Highway on the east side of Duluth. There is a pavilion and place where you can park your car for a picnic. Often people just stay in their cars to look at the lake. For obvious reasons, it is a popular necking spot. In the winter, the parkway is blocked off to car traffic, but pedestrians often walk the road or wander down to the lake to explore the rocky shoreline. On this night, it appeared deserted. No cars were parked at the barricade, and no one was visible on foot. I walked in a quarter of a mile, then down to the shoreline, and plunked myself on a rock. I had not planned this and found myself wondering why I had come. I have lived in Duluth all of my life and whenever I have needed time to think, I have always gravitated to the shores of Lake Superior.

Each time I sit on her shores, I see a different lake. Sometimes it is icy and windy, and sometimes hot and still. On this day, it was cold and gusty. The waves were seven feet high by the time they came crashing into the rocky shore. As they hit, they created a splash that reached another ten feet higher. Where I sat, I could feel a heavy mist carried on the wind. As each wave crashed with a cadenced rhythm, it brought to mind a story one of my Native American client's parents told me a long time ago.

He said that waves are produced when the body of water dreams. The dreams come in waves throughout the night and leave a little of themselves behind to change the world. Then they cleanse themselves on the shore and return to the depths. I sat there thinking about the waves and of my dreams. I could see the historic Duluth lift bridge from my vantage point, and the Blatnik Bridge behind it. They were both lit up with what looked like Christmas lights.

I don't know how long I sat there, but I became aware of movement twenty feet to my left. I turned slowly to see a doe and two fawns. They must have tiptoed their way to the water, and they were drinking from a shallow pool left behind in the rocks by the crashing waves. I sat there for ten minutes more just watching them. They seemed unaware of my presence. I was cold but transfixed. When they had their fill, they slowly walked into the woods. I sensed that the deer knew that the lake was dreaming.

I slowly unlocked my frozen joints and made my way to the Range Rover. I wished for a remote starter because I was cold. You're getting soft, Jo, I told myself. The short walk seemed to take forever. I was feeling old. When I finally reached the car, I glanced in the mirror, and my eyelashes were covered in ice. I had also totally forgotten about my nose injury. It had a nice, dark scab. Why hadn't anyone asked me about my nose today? I guess things were really bad for folks at work. As I started the Rover, I thought of Zoey. I was frozen to the core, but the thought of her warmed me.

Just as I was easing back onto the Scenic Highway, she called.

"Jo, it's Zoey."

I smiled when I heard her voice.

"Hi, Zoey." I'm not a big conversationalist on the phone.

"Where are you?"

"On my way home."

"Wanna join me for dinner?"

"I was just down watching the lake, and I got soaked."

"We can do it without clothes." She laughed out loud. So did I.

"We usually do."

"We should try it with clothes some time."

"I'm game."

"I just bet you are."

I was making a U-turn before I answered. "Let me see if I can get K. and D. to take my dogs. I'll call you right back."

Kathy was not home, but Donna agreed to go get the pups. I thanked her profusely. When I reached Zoey's, I had thawed considerably but was still wet. She ushered me straight into the shower and collected my wet clothes. When I emerged, we sat down to a dinner of potato leek soup and garlic bread. I was adorned in her sweats from head to toe. It felt odd for me to wear someone else's clothing, but I tried to appear flexible. I was going to have to keep a spare set of clothing at her house for emergencies. At least we were close to the same size.

Chapter 32

HALFWAY THROUGH DINNER, my cell phone rang. It was the security company calling to tell me that my alarm had tripped. I told them I was pretty sure it was a friend picking up my dogs, but I would call them right back. I phoned Donna. She was home, had picked up the dogs twenty-five minutes before, and said that she hadn't gone near the house. I called the security company back and told them it was not a false alarm. They called 911, and Zoey and I hopped into the Range Rover.

The Duluth Township squad was parked with its nose facing out in my driveway. Officer Shilhon was nowhere in sight. Lights were on in the house. I wondered what to do now. They didn't tell me about this part in my orientation for the alarm. Zoey and I cautiously entered through the front door. It was closed but unlocked.

"Dan?" I said aloud.

There was no response. I motioned to Zoey with the universal sign for silence, index finger to the lips, and backed out of the door with her in tow. We tiptoed out to the squad to have a look inside and to access the radio.

"Dispatch, this is Jo Spence. I'm at my residence."

"Dispatch to Spence. Do you know the location of Officer Shilhon?"

"Negative. That's why I'm checking with you. His squad's at my residence, but he's nowhere in sight. I called out for him inside the house, but he didn't respond. The lights are on, and the door is open. I didn't go all the way in."

"Are you in any danger right now?"

"No."

"I'm sending backup as we speak."

Just as she said that, I could see someone inside the house walking toward the front door. He appeared to be much shorter than Dan.

"Suspect is in the house. We have to leave. Please hurry with help."

Zoey had been standing next to me on the driver's side of the car. I exited, eased the door shut, and pulled her with me into the woods. There were no keys in the squad car and the keys to my car were inside the house. I had hung my keys on the hook just inside the door out of habit. Habits—they get me in trouble.

"Zoey, do you remember how to get to Kathy and Donna's from here?"

"Yes, but I'm not leaving you. Who do you think that is, and what happened to Officer Shilhon?"

"If Dan is in there and he's injured or whatever, the suspect heard us on the radio. He knows backup is on the way."

"Let's both go, then."

"No, he may follow us. I can't risk it. He's probably armed."

"I'm not leaving you here."

I was filled with the conflicting emotions of wanting desperately to protect Zoey and feeling in awe of her courage. I also realized the power of what we could do together, not just in this instance, but in our future. Something shifted in me, and I realized we could be an awesome force. Even though Zoey and I might have been risking our lives, I somehow knew that everything would be fine.

I squeezed her hand and said, "You are a stubborn shit, aren't you?"

She flashed me a scared smile.

The intruder inside my house was opening the front door. Under the entryway light, the man I recognized as Drift or Tre was clearly visible.

"Shit," stumbled out of my mouth in a whisper. He just stood there listening. I thought I heard a faint siren in the distance. I called Nate's cell, and he answered right away. I whispered, "I can't talk, tell me what you know." I was careful to keep the light from the phone turned away from Drift.

"Are you OK?"

"Yes."

"Lou has been shot. He's in the hospital, but he should be all right. Lou thought he wounded his attacker. Drift should be bleeding. I'm ten minutes away. Hang on. Don't mess with him!"

Drift started to move, and I closed the phone. He was moving slowly and walking with a distinct limp. I nudged Zoey, and we walked farther into the woods, heading north from my house. The snow was deep, so I thought it best to trample through it rather than take the path. The going would be tough for him. I wasn't sure about the extent of his injury, but I was banking on it slowing him down. The forest is much denser behind my house, and the trees are a good seventy-five years older than the ones growing near the clearing. It was dark, and I had the advantage of knowing every inch of the land. We crossed my property behind the house and doubled back. I wanted to end up in the shop that occupied the back third of my garage. I practically lived in this woodworking shop when Kathy and I were building the house. We occasionally tinker in there now, on small projects. I was confident I could navigate it in the dark. It took nearly ten minutes to make our way to the shop door. We had stopped from time to time to make sure he was still tracking us.

Zoey entered the shop first, and I guided her over to the door leading to the main part of the garage. Placing her hand on the light switch, I told her to flip it when he opened the door. I grabbed a huge crowbar from the supply of tools, as well as a plumber's wrench. I guided the wrench to Zoey's free hand and gave her a squeeze. I then walked over to the door and waited. I heard no sirens.

We waited for what seemed like an hour. I pictured Drift with his greasy blond hair. I thought about the seven lives he had taken, and my heart was pounding nearly out of my chest. I heard footsteps outside the door, followed by silence. The doorknob turned, and the door cracked open. I waited again for him to walk into the shop. He pushed the door open, and I yelled, "Now." The lights went on, and I swung. I felt the crowbar hit with a thud. I had aimed for his head. He groaned and tumbled back into the door, forcing it closed. He was on the floor with the gun still in his hand, but he wasn't moving. Zoey came flying across the shop and stood on his gun hand while still holding the wrench. I was in awe.

I kicked the gun out of his hand and picked it up, handing it to Zoey. His face had begun to swell, and he was still not moving. I asked Zoey, "Do you know how to use that thing?"

"Sure do. The safety's off."

"I'll ask you about that later. I'm going to get some rope."

I went into the main part of the garage and retrieved a hefty length of rope and my handcuffs from the Range Rover. I pushed Drift over onto his stomach and cuffed him behind his back. Then I tied his legs together and secured him to the table saw.

I walked over to Zoey and looked at her. Her composure gave way. She gently put the gun on the workbench and crumpled into my arms. We both sat down, leaned against the workbench, and just stared at him. The Duluth squads finally pulled up. Nate was the first to enter, gun first.

I said, "Look at what happened to the last guy who brought a gun into my house."

He just stood there stunned.

"What the …? This isn't what I meant by 'don't mess with him.'"

"Like we had a choice."

He holstered his gun and felt Drift's neck for a pulse. He was alive. Another officer called for an ambulance, and Nate untied our captive. Drift had not regained consciousness.

Two cops guarded him while Nate helped Zoey to her wobbly feet and escorted us into the house. He sat us both down at the breakfast bar and searched the house. He radioed for ambulance assistance. I had totally forgotten about Shilhon. Nate said he appeared to be unconscious in the bedroom with a softball bat lying by his head. That meant that he had been unconscious for over half an hour. An ambulance came, and the paramedics gently rolled Shilhon onto a backboard and then onto a gurney. Nate came back into the kitchen, and I brewed a pot of decaf. We filled him in on the night's events.

Although he could see that we were physically healthy, he offered to stay at the house in case we were traumatized by what we had been through. We both declined, and I called Kathy and Donna. They brought the dogs over and just sat with us for hours.

Later, as Zoey and I drifted off to sleep, without thinking I murmured, "I love you." I heard the same in reply.

Chapter 33

I CALLED LOU the following morning. He was quite drugged. He had been shot in the upper left portion of his chest just above his heart. The bullet had traveled through him without doing any real damage. He wasn't feeling that lucky, though. He would have to do physical therapy for his shoulder and would suffer a long stint away from work. Lou needed and loved his work. I told him I'd visit him soon.

As soon as I hung up, I received an incoming collect call from my dad. He was still on the cruise but had used the ship's internet service to check the Duluth news. He was horrified by what he had read but also relieved to learn that I was alive. The newspaper article was entitled, "Head of Juvenile Probation and Professor Foil Killer." He lectured me for ten minutes, vowed his fatherly love, then went back to lecturing for another five minutes. He wasn't much interested in what I had to say, so I just listened.

As soon as I hung up, I got a call from my Chief. He was setting up a critical incident debriefing and offered to involve Zoey. I told him that she was still sleeping, and I would get back to him. He had no intention of letting me get out of this. I finally accepted, but said it would have to be at my house. I needed to reclaim it. I also told him I needed a couple of weeks off.

I hung up the phone, unplugged it, and went back to bed with Zoey.

She had her teaching assistant cover her classes, and we spent another day together just hanging out. At 10 A.M., Sam showed up, and I introduced her to Zoey. She was clearly impressed, jokingly offering her a job. She also informed me that the profile had come back on Tre/Drift.

"Drift saw himself as a professional. He had totally adopted the image of hired killer with a definite set of rules he operated by. One of those rules was that if he missed a hit, he would keep coming back until he was successful. The reason he didn't kill Shilhon was that he never killed unnecessarily."

"A principled killer?"

"Exactly."

She also said that Shilhon was coming out of a massive concussion but would lose no functioning. Sam left with the promise of a lunch date soon, and she shook Zoey's hand and mine with respect.

By the time the weekend rolled around, we were sane enough to call Kathy and Donna for a game of hearts. This time, we held out for my house.

Preview of Jen Wright's Forthcoming Novel:

Big Noise

Chapter One

They settled onto the floor of their rented cabin for a cup of French- pressed dark roast. The wood stove was doing a slow burn on two birch logs that their hosts had cut and split by hand. Though they were still quite early on in their new relationship, their respective jobs had been interfering with both the quality and quantity of time that they had to spend with each other. Jo's position as Juvenile Probation Supervisor in Duluth, and Zoey's tenure-track professorship kept them both quite occupied.

Zoey had suggested to Jo on the ride up that it would be nice for them to reconnect and talk after a hectic week. Jo, on the other hand, had found herself wanting to spend the entire two weeks of their wilderness vacation in bed.

She knew that she would have a tough time letting go of work because of her tendency to focus way too much on juvenile delinquency and on crime in general. She couldn't go to a store without eyeing the place for shoplifters, or leave an item in plain sight in her car, fearing that it might tempt would-be thieves. She even found herself going on rants to her friends about their own lack of security in their homes. She hoped that this deep-woods retreat would be just what she needed to get away from it all.

Jo prompted Zoey to fill her in on what progress she had made in writing up her research project. As she listened to her lover begin to speak, Jo couldn't imagine finding such research fun—all that data crunching—but she couldn't fail to notice how Zoey really brightened when she talked about it. The University's Health Center where Zoey worked proved to be a perfect place to collect the data because semi-voluntary clients walked in each and every day. Zoey had been working on the project with their mutual good friend Donna, a nurse practitioner at the U. They had screened for the mental health needs of the students coming in, regardless of what ailed them.

"As suspected, we found a high number of students with anxiety, depression, and some more serious disorders that would not have been uncovered had they not been screened. We also tracked how many students accepted help following the screenings."

Before she had finished telling Jo about her findings, Zoey was suddenly interrupted by Jo wrestling her down flat on the floor. More accurately, Zoey feigned resistance to Jo wrestling her down on the floor.

Once she had her pinned, Jo exclaimed, "You know what that academic stuff does to me. You've gone too far this time."

"What are you going to do about it?"

Jo decided to let her actions speak for themselves and began undoing Zoey's purple flannel shirt one button at a time. Again Zoey feigned resistance. Jo had to move her knees, which were immobilizing Zoey's arms, in order to relieve Zoey of her shirtsleeves, and Zoey turned the tables by bucking her back up and then pinning Jo down.

"OK, tough guy, what are you gonna do now?" she intoned.

She began slowly unzipping Jo's fleece until she had it completely open.

Just when it looked like she was facing the same awkward predicament Jo had been in, she simply pulled Jo's bra up, exposing her breasts. She then took Jo's shirt and bra completely off. She lowered herself so that she was nearly touching her, stopped and sat upright, putting her arms up in the air and flexing her biceps.

"I am so in control here."

She got up, went over to the loft stairway and motioned to Jo with the universal "come here" finger curl and began unzipping her jeans. Jo sprung up, causing Zoey to squeal and run up the ladder with Jo in fast pursuit. By the time Jo reached the top of the ladder, Zoey had managed to shred every thread of clothing and was lying on top of the bed naked waiting for her.

Jo slipped out of her remaining garments and kneeled beside Zoey, nuzzling her nose in under her chin and into her neck, and began nibbling on the lobe of her ear. Jo had recently discovered that this was an erogenous zone for Zoey, and she was intent on exploiting it as far as she could. Zoey reached up and pulled Jo onto her so that she was straddled, willingly exposing her neck. Jo began alternately kissing and nibbling her way from one ear to the next and then down. Zoey arched her back in anticipation of Jo reaching her breast, but Jo teased her until she let out a soft plea. As soon as Jo's mouth reached her breast, Jo's hand began reaching lower. She moved in a circular motion with her mouth and hand until Zoey cried out.

Zoey was sweat covered when she reached for Jo, who by then ached for Zoey to be inside of her and wouldn't tolerate any teasing. Zoey lingered just long enough for Jo to reach for her hand and whisper, "I need you now."

Zoey moved in powerful rhythms that shook right through Jo until she was spent and then spent again. They held each other for a time and then descended the ladder naked. Jo felt laden with pleasure as she slowly walked to the sink and retrieved a bowl, filling it partway with cold water. She added hot water from the wood stove kettle and found a clean towel under the sink. She guided Zoey down on a towel in front of the fire and cleaned every inch of her front and back.

"I guess I could live without a shower. Do you think this is how Sandy and ReAnn stay clean?"

"I dare you to ask them."

She laid her head back and in a childish tone said, "Oh, no—I'm not asking them—you ask them."

Sandy and ReAnn lived thirty miles north of Jo's home in the Valley in a community called Big Noise. While Jo considered herself to be "country folk," living fifteen miles outside of Duluth, her idea of roughing it paled in comparison to the folks who called Big Noise their home.

Big Noise houses several hundred residents in a forty-mile area. It was settled during the logging boom in the early 1900s by loggers who, when they came out of the woods after a day of work, were drawn to the tavern by the noise. The name Big Noise just stuck. Most of the residents owned several hundred acres and lived in rustic homes constructed by the early loggers.

Sandy and ReAnn's cabin was just such a homestead. They had built the guest cabin on their property primarily because they love building things. Evidence of that passion lay in the several hand-hewn buildings scattered in what they called their "Compound."

Closest to the main cabin was the woodshed. As large as the size of most two-car garages, it was built almost entirely of slab wood. The spaces between slabs served as draft to dry out the wood so that it could be easily ignited and burned efficiently. The shed also housed a four-wheeler with a plow on it as well as a garden tractor. The building closest to the guest cabin was a garage/shop. In this traditional stick-built structure, the land owners housed their vehicles and a substantial shop. Most of the tools in the shop were 1950s-era Craftsmans. A few newer brands stuck out like sore thumbs.

Just south of the main cabin, a large screen house full of comfortable wicker furniture and a huge hammock beckoned cabin guests. Behind the woodshed stood a sauna, with vertically placed cedar boards as siding that had been allowed to naturally gray over time. Last but not least important, an outhouse sat apart from all of the other structures, and it also featured naturally gray cedar siding. All of the structures including the guest cabin had matching green metal roofs.

Sandy and ReAnn only rented the guest cabin to friends and friends of friends. Jo and Zoey had reserved it for the two full weeks of Zoey's winter break. As a tenure track professor at Duluth University, she spent a chunk of her time preparing for her classes and writing. She enjoyed the work, so it really wasn't a hardship for her. Jo had no such strings tethering her to work during her paid vacations, but she didn't enjoy the academic perk of having the summers off, either. They had not had to face this as a couple at this stage in their relationship, but Jo dreaded the thought of having to get up and trek off to work, while Zoey lingered in bed.

The fire was still going, easily heating the small one-room lofted log cabin they would call home for the next couple of weeks. Sandy had stocked their wood supply inside and out. Their hostesses had filled the little gas fridge to capacity as well, and Jo and Zoey had already made several batches of French pressed coffee by heating water on the propane stove. Zoey, well aware of Jo's coffee addiction, had packed a formidable supply—knowing that they couldn't possibly venture anywhere without the makings for good, strong coffee.

Even though she joked about living without a shower after her sponge bath, Zoey still hadn't really adjusted to the idea of being out in the woods without running water. Jo made a silent vow to herself to come up with more little surprises for Zoey in relation to this issue.

After drying off, Jo and Zoey gathered all of their winterwear and ventured just outside the cabin door to the Cloquet River for a snowshoe adventure. Zoey loved that she could maneuver her large old-fashioned snowshoes around downed trees, large boulders, and pockets of open water. For a woman who had moved to northern Minnesota less than six months earlier, she showed no signs of running from the cold and snow. Her bomber-style hat was completely covered, and her eyelashes cradled several delicate flakes. She stopped and looked around with amazement at the beauty of this new place.

In true Zoey fashion, she just had to try her hand at being in the lead, a task usually reserved for experience river trackers. Jo followed close behind, amazed at her lover's apparent intuitive ability to navigate the river. She certainly hadn't gained any of this knowledge in her former home in the New Mexico desert.

Jo pictured their adventure through Zoey's eyes. Cedar trees grew stubbornly out of rock formations bordering the river. A white blanket covered many of the large white pine branches that hovered over them. Their breathing produced short bursts of steam.

While Zoey was dressed perfectly for the snowshoe hike, Jo knew from watching her fill in her wardrobe over the previous few months that she had worked quite hard at it. When she made the trek up north she hadn't owned any jackets heavier than a windbreaker. She had acquired quite a bit of gear, but she had not yet adjusted to the casual way most northerners cared for their outerwear. She rarely wore anything twice without washing it, and Jo even caught her ironing her flannel shirts. Jo chuckled as she gently pointed out that if she was going to iron flannel, she better not leave a crease or everyone would know.

Zoey knew on some level that she still stood out as an interloper because she was just too well put together. She usually looked like she was modeling for an outdoor magazine or that she never actually used the clothing for any real activities. Jo found it all totally adorable, but silently wondered how Zoey would adjust to their little rented cabin in the woods with no washing machine or iron.

Jo had equal but opposite dress habits, and she found herself wondering what Zoey thought of them. Wearing virtually the same outfit every day for work or play, Jo owned twelve button-down Pendleton shirts and twelve permanent press, khaki pants. When her work clothing became worn, she rotated it into her casual clothing. She had, however, brought some fleece shirts and pants in honor of their rustic adventure.

Where the river narrowed for a curve, the snowshoers were nearly encircled in snow-covered branches. Zoey knew better than to stand under such a branch, as it would afford her lover the opportunity to give it a shove, causing snow to fall on her head and down her neck.

As they entered a clearing with no trees overhead, Zoey slowed, moved into a large circle, and turned to face Jo. She inched her snowshoes in closer, placing one in between Jo's legs and the other to one side, and leaned in. She knew Jo couldn't possibly move without toppling both of them over into a snowshoe/human heap. She flashed her wickedest grin and moved in for a kiss. Jo could feel her smiling as her warm lips began to melt into her. She gave in easily and fully to Zoey as her entire body warmed over with pleasure. The warmth easily lasted for the mile return hike back to their rented cabin bordering the river.

Jen Wright lives and writes in Clover Valley,
Minnesota. She welcomes reader feedback about
Killer Storm, her first novel. You may correspond
with her at beingjenwright@juno.com.

Clover Valley Press, LLC, is a new women's publishing company. We specialize in producing quality books by women writers of the northland.

Our mission goes beyond encouraging female writers to find their voices—we help them to join the human conversation through publishing.

For author guidelines or to purchase copies of our books, go to www.clovervalleypress.com.

CLOVER
VALLEY
PRESS

Printed in the United States
76271LV00002B/1-99

9 780979 488306

O R M
OXFORD RESPIRATORY MEDI

369 0291090

Asthma

DATE DUE

20/3/13	
12/3/14	
4·6·15	
4/11/15	
24/11/15	
12/10/16	
21/2/17	
13/11/18	
2 7 NOV 2018	

▶ Except where otherwise stated, drug doses and recommendations are for the non-pregnant adult who is not breast-feeding.

O R M L

OXFORD RESPIRATORY MEDICINE LIBRARY

Asthma
Second edition

Edited by

Graeme P. Currie

MBChB, DCH, Pg Dip M Ed, MD, FRCP
Consultant Respiratory Physician,
Aberdeen Royal Infimary,
Aberdeen, Scotland, UK

John F. W. Baker

MBChB, BA (Hons)
Foundation Doctor,
Aberdeen Royal Infirmary,
Aberdeen, Scotland, UK

OXFORD
UNIVERSITY PRESS

OXFORD
UNIVERSITY PRESS

Great Clarendon Street, Oxford, OX2 6DP,
United Kingdom

Oxford University Press is a department of the University of Oxford.
It furthers the University's objective of excellence in research, scholarship,
and education by publishing worldwide. Oxford is a registered trade mark of
Oxford University Press in the UK and in certain other countries

© Oxford University Press 2012

The moral rights of the authors have been asserted

First edition published in 2008
Second edition published in 2012

Impression: 1

British Library Cataloguing in Publication Data
Data available

Library of Congress Cataloging in Publication Data
Library of Congress Control Number: 2012931712

ISBN 978-0-19-963891-8

Printed in Great Britain by
Ashford Colour Press Ltd, Gosport, Hampshire